Millie's Faithful Heart

BOOK FOUR
of the
*A Life of Faith:
Millie Keith*
Series

Based on the beloved books by
Martha Finley

MCP
Mission City Press

Franklin, Tennessee

Book Four of the *A Life of Faith: Millie Keith* Series

Millie's Faithful Heart
Copyright © 2002, Mission City Press, Inc. All Rights Reserved.

Published by Mission City Press, Inc.

This book is based on the *Mildred Keith* novels written by Martha Finley and first published in 1876 by Dodd, Mead & Company.

Adaptation Written by:	Kersten Hamilton
Cover & Interior Design:	Richmond & Williams
Cover Photography:	Michelle Grisco Photography
Typesetting:	BookSetters

Unless otherwise indicated, all Scripture references are from the Holy Bible, New International Version (NIV). Copyright © 1973, 1978, 1984 by International Bible Society. Used by permission of Zondervan Publishing House, Grand Rapids, MI. All rights reserved.

Millie Keith and *A Life of Faith* are trademarks of Mission City Press, Inc.

For more information, write to Mission City Press at P.O. Box 681913, Franklin, Tennessee 37068-1913, or visit our Web Site at:

www.alifeoffaith.com

Library of Congress Catalog Card Number: 2001092284
Finley, Martha
    Millie's Faithful Heart
    Book Four of the *A Life of Faith: Millie Keith* Series
    ISBN: 1-928749-12-7

Printed in the United States of America
2 3 4 5 6 7 8 — 07 06 05 04 03

DEDICATION

This book is
dedicated to
the memory of
MARTHA FINLEY
1828—1909

*Martha Finley was a woman of God
clearly committed to advancing the cause of Christ
through stories of people who sought
to reflect Christian character in everyday life.
Although written in an era very different from ours,
her works still inspire both young and old
to seek to know and follow the living God.*

*I*n *Millie's Faithful Heart*, the fourth of the *A Life of Faith: Millie Keith* Series, you are invited to continue learning about the past as you grow in faith with Millie. Our story resumes in November of 1836 on the southern plantation of Horace Dinsmore, Sr., Millie's uncle. Millie, who is a staunch abolitionist, has traveled to the South for health reasons, but now, ironically, finds herself the owner of a young slave girl named Laylie.

The stories of Millie Keith, known formerly as the *Mildred Keith* novels, were published in 1876, eight years after the well-known *Elsie Dinsmore* books were first introduced. Martha Finley, the creator of both characters, wrote the stories of Elsie's second cousin, Millie Keith, as a companion to the Elsie novels.

This book is an adaptation of the original Mildred Keith story. In rewriting the books for modern readers, the Christian message has been strengthened, the plot has been enhanced, new characters have been added, old characters have been more fully developed, historical information has been added, and other changes have been made to enhance the reader's involvement with and enjoyment of the story.

Millie Keith is a model of courage and conviction. Although she lives in a time period different than our own, her desire to be faithful to the Lord is an inspiration to people of any era.

⤬ SOCIAL DIFFERENCES IN MILLIE'S DAY ⤬

Although there were both rich Christians and poor Christians in America in 1836, their lives were far more segregated than the lives of rich and poor today, and the South

was perhaps the most socially segregated portion of America.

The antebellum South was very different socially from Millie's home on the wild frontier. Families such as the Dinsmores had lived on their land for generations, many since before the Revolutionary War. Although the working-class people of the South lived very much as Millie did in Pleasant Plains, Indiana, the wealthy people of the South spent their time enjoying music, art, hunting, dancing, and other forms of entertainment. Wealthy plantation owners considered manual labor beneath them and believed that true gentlemen should never work hard enough to produce sweat. Most of the aristocracy considered the separation of classes very important. People who had earned their fortunes instead of inheriting them were considered of a lower class, and simply were not welcome in the best society. They were called "codfish aristocracy," a reference to the fishing industry in which many late eighteenth- and early nine-teenth-century fortunes were made.

In the lower classes—whether they lived in the North, the South, or on the frontier—everyone worked at building their homes and businesses and keeping their families in good order. Women and children labored along with the men. Young women were expected to know how to cook, sew, do laundry, grow food in the garden, tend the sick and wounded, chop wood, shoot, and even dress game or slaughter livestock for food. These tasks might have shocked and dismayed wealthy women, but a poor man looked for a wife who was not afraid to work hard all day. The average woman in 1836 rose before the sun to feed, clothe, and care for her family, and her work went on long

after the sun went down and the men had ceased their labor.

In the East and the South, a well-off young lady spent her childhood years studying things that would be useful in courtship and genteel society: needlepoint, French, poetry, music, art, and proper manners and etiquette. A girl was trained to be a gracious hostess to her husband's guests. At first glance, this seems much simpler than slopping hogs, quilting, and chopping wood. But ladies of the upper class did not have much freedom.

The list of things an upper class woman could not do in polite company was seemingly endless. She could not ask direct questions such as, "What is the time?" She could not touch the person to whom she was speaking with her hand, and she could not wink, blink, or squint her eyes, look steadily at a person, tap her feet or hand to keep rhythm with the music, or adjust her hair. The rules went on and on. Even her topics of conversation were limited. Ladies were simply not expected to understand complicated subjects such as science, economics, or politics.

COURTSHIP

While working-class girls might go with young men to corn huskings, barn dances, or other community parties, dating as we know it did not exist for high society girls in the 1830s. Young ladies from genteel families were rarely without a chaperone, usually a grim older aunt or the girl's mother, who would go with her to parties, the theater, and social events. The chaperone would even sit with the young people in parlor visits.

Families were concerned that their children did not marry out of their social circle, and books were written to

help ladies recognize and turn down proposals from young men who were seeking to win their fortunes by marrying an heiress. For the romantically challenged of the appropriate social status, books of Valentine poems, called Valentine "writers," were imported from England. These writers were filled with verses that less-than-poetic young men could copy onto gilt-edged paper to impress their valentine. Just in case the young lady was not inclined to write poetry either, a rhyming answer was included that she could copy and send back—provided, of course, that she had her own copy of the book.

After a young man had spent ample time with a girl and her family, he would approach her father with a request for her hand in marriage. The young man could expect to be questioned about his fortune or his business and his ability to support a wife. If he was found suitable, he was given permission to approach the young lady with an offer of marriage. However, in high society, even romance moved slowly. Many courtships were done by correspondence, and many couples waited years before they wed.

Young women of many social classes kept diaries of their courtships, and courting couples exchanged love letters and tokens such as rings, old coins, lockets, and sketches. Proposals were frequently carried out by letter, and a young woman expected to be asked more than once by the same suitor. She needed time to consider, and he, by asking more than once, proved his determination to win her. A young man would not be put off by one, two, or even three refusals of his love.

For young ladies of a good family, courtship and romance followed strict rules. A young lady could not speak with a young man until they were properly introduced by a mutual

acquaintance; if they were introduced at a ball or formal dance for the purpose of dancing, they could not speak again until they were properly and formally introduced at a later date. Although a young lady could not speak to a gentleman she did not know, she could send messages in code with her fan across the room — or to a gentleman sitting beside her:

> Fan slow: I am already engaged
> Fan fast: I am single
> Fan with right hand in front of face: follow me
> Fan with left hand in front of face: leave me alone
> Open and shut: kiss me
> Fan wide open: I love you
> Drawing it across your forehead: someone is watching us
> Touch your right cheek: yes
> Touch your left cheek: no

Still, with all the strict rules and strange courting rituals, even the most proper and sheltered, wealthy young people did meet and fall in love just as often as their poorer cousins.

KEITH FAMILY TREE

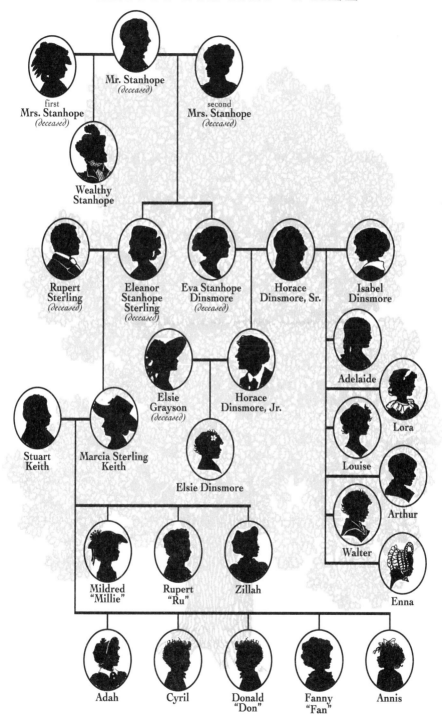

Setting

$\mathcal{O}$ur story begins in November of 1836 at Roselands, the Dinsmore plantation, where Millie Keith has been sent for the winter because of her weakened lungs.

Characters in Pleasant Plains, Indiana

 The Keith Family

Stuart Keith–the father of the Keith family; a respected attorney-at-law.

Marcia Keith–the mother of the Keith family and the step-niece of Aunt Wealthy Stanhope.

The Keith children:

> **Mildred Eleanor ("Millie")**–age 15
> **Rupert ("Ru")**–age 14
> **Zillah**–age 12
> **Adah**–age 11
> **Cyril** and **Donald ("Don")**–age 10, twin boys
> **Fanny ("Fan")**–age 8
> **Annis**–age 4

Wealthy Stanhope–a woman in her late 50s; Marcia's step-aunt who raised her from infancy; step-aunt to Horace Dinsmore, Jr.; she lives in Lansdale, Ohio.

∽ Friends in Pleasant Plains ∽

Millie's Girlfriends:
>**Rhoda Jane Lightcap**–age 17
>**Claudina Chetwood**–age 16
>**Lucilla Grange**–age 17
>**Helen Monocker**–age 18

Reverend Matthew and **Celestia Ann Lord**–a local minister and his wife.

Damaris Drybread–a local teacher, age 25.

Nicholas Ransquate–a local young man, age 28.

Characters at Roselands Plantation

∽ The Dinsmore Household ∽

Horace Dinsmore, Sr.–uncle to Marcia Keith.

Isabel Dinsmore–second wife of Horace Dinsmore, Sr.

The Dinsmore children:
>**Adelaide**–age 12
>**Lora**–age 10
>**Louise**–age 8
>**Arthur**–age 6
>**Walter**–age 4
>**Enna**–age 2

Jonati–a slave nursemaid to the Dinsmore children.

Miss Worth–governess to the Dinsmore children.

Mrs. Brown–housekeeper at Roselands.

Phoebe—cook at Roselands.

∞ OTHERS ∞

Laylie–a slave, age 10.

Luke–a slave, Laylie's brother, age 15.

Otis Lochneer–age 19, friend of the Dinsmores.

Mr. and Mrs. Landreth–a wealthy middle-aged couple.

Charles Landreth–age 20, friend of the Dinsmore family; nephew to the Landreths.

Mrs. Travilla–owner of Ion plantation.

Old Rachel–an elderly slave woman belonging to Mrs. Travilla.

Horace Dinsmore, Jr.–age 23, the son of Horace Dinsmore, Sr. and his first wife, Eva.

> **Elsie**–age 4, the daughter of Horace, Jr. and Elsie Grayson (deceased).

Aunt Chloe–Elsie Dinsmore's nursemaid at Viamede, the Louisiana plantation where Elsie has lived since her birth.

Mrs. Murray–housekeeper at Viamede.

Mr. and Mrs. Breandan–parents of Isabel Dinsmore and owners of Meadshead Plantation.

Ronald Borse–head overseer of the slaves at Meadshead Plantation.

Miz Opal, Miz Ruth, Miz Magnolia, Mrs. "Dearest" Bliss–Four middle-aged cousins from North Carolina who Millie met, along with their uncle Colonel Peabody, on a steamboat trip to Pittsburgh. Mrs. Bliss and her husband, Mr. Blessed Bliss, own a funeral parlor in North Carolina.

CHAPTER

1

A Sneak and a Thief

For there is nothing hidden that will not be disclosed, and nothing concealed that will not be known or brought out into the open.

LUKE 8:17

A Sneak and a Thief

I'm a slave owner! Millie Keith realized suddenly with horror. *I have just bought a child by promising to play the piano! Now what do I do, Lord?*

Was it just a month ago that Millie was standing in front of her Bible study group in Pleasant Plains, Indiana, teaching that slavery was wrong? Coming to Roselands, her Uncle Horace's plantation, had seemed like an excellent way to learn the truth about the South, about slavery. *I want to go home, Lord. So what if Dr. Chetwood recommended a milder climate for my lungs? He has been wrong before. This is a horrible place. No, Aunt Isabel is a horrible person. She has used my feelings about slavery against me quite cleverly. If I agree to play the piano at Aunt Isabel's parties, then Laylie will belong to me. If I don't buy the child, she will be sent back to Meadshead to work endless hours in the fields.* Her aunt's perfume hung in the hallway where she had been standing only moments before, thick as cobwebs on the damp air. *How could Isabel have known my heart so well?* Millie shivered. *My diary! She couldn't have read it, could she?*

"Here you are!" Millie jumped at the sound of Louise's voice. "Come to the nursery and tell us a story," the young girl demanded. "Jonati and Miss Worth and Father are trying to get a peppermint stick out of Enna's nose, and Mother said you would tell us one."

"A peppermint stick? How . . . ? Never mind. I can't come right now; there is something I must do," replied Millie. She started toward her room, but Louise caught her hand. "You *have* to. Mother said she has a headache. She said you would tell us a story. Mother *said*!"

Millie's Faithful Heart

Is this part of the bargain? Do I have to do everything Aunt Isabel orders? Millie's head was still spinning as she allowed Louise to lead her down the carpeted hall. Long before they reached the nursery, she could hear Enna's shrieks coming from Miss Worth's apartments, where they had apparently carried the child.

Once Millie was safely in the nursery and the door was shut, Louise went to stand beside her sister Lora. The two girls wore matching ribbons and bows. Even the pouts on their lips matched, and said very plainly that they were not happy about being left alone. Walter, who was only four, looked worried as Millie picked him up and turned to Adelaide, the oldest, who had her arms crossed and was glaring at her brother Arthur. Arthur was very busy looking innocent, which meant he was guilty of something. In the short time that Millie had been at Roselands, she had learned that Arthur only possessed two looks: one sly, which meant he was planning something, and one innocent, which meant he had just committed a crime.

"How did baby Enna get a peppermint stick?" Millie asked.

"We don't know," Adelaide said, still glaring. "But Arthur was in the corner with her."

"I didn't tell her to put it up her nose!" snarled Arthur.

"But you didn't stop her either," said Adelaide, her frown growing darker.

"She puts everything up her nose!" Arthur said. "You know she does. Why does everyone think *I* am the guilty one? I'm not the only one around here who gets into trouble, you know."

"That's enough of that, I think," Millie said. "At least if you want to hear a story."

4

A Sneak and a Thief

"I don't want a story," Arthur said defiantly. "I want a book."

Millie looked at him in surprise. She had never seen Arthur with a book in his hand.

"I want *Robin Hood*," he demanded.

"Do you have a copy in the nursery?" Millie asked, forcing herself to be pleasant.

"No," Arthur said. "It's in Father's library. We'll go with you to get it."

"All right," Millie agreed. "One chapter of *Robin Hood*. And then I have things I must do."

Enna's screams had quieted, and Millie assumed the peppermint stick had successfully been removed. She wished that Miss Worth or Jonati would appear and take the children in hand, but the door to Miss Worth's apartments remained closed, with only sniffles and sobs seeping through. Millie sighed in resignation and led the children down the hall.

Uncle Horace's library was his refuge. He had given Millie free reign of the room and permission to borrow any book, but the Persian rug on the library floor was strange territory to the Dinsmore children. Their father called them into his inner sanctum only if they were in need of discipline or reproof, and even at that, not nearly as often as he might. Lora, Louise, and Walter stayed outside the door peeking in, but Adelaide and Arthur boldly followed Millie inside.

"It's a green book," Arthur said, "with a picture on the cover." The description was not a great deal of help, as there were hundreds of volumes in the room. Uncle Horace had his books arranged by subject, and Millie searched the legends shelf, but to no avail.

"Are you sure your father has a copy of *Robin Hood*?" Millie asked.

"Someone has probably taken it," Arthur said, giving Adelaide a sly look. "We have a thief in the house."

"It wasn't me," Adelaide said.

"They whip thieves," Arthur said gaily.

"Let's read this one instead," said Millie, picking up a book of fairy tales by the Brothers Grimm. She had no desire to discuss anyone being whipped—especially not after seeing Luke's back. For the crime of being a few minutes late to the fields to work, Laylie's brother had been lashed to a post and beaten until his back was nothing but raw wounds and ribbons of flesh. Because he was a borrowed slave, Uncle Horace had not even been informed about the beating.

Millie, carrying the book, led the troop back to the nursery. She settled them on the plush carpet and began the story of Cinderella.

The invitation to the prince's ball had just arrived when Jonati appeared with a puffy-eyed Enna. The baby insisted on sitting on Millie's lap for the rest of the story. Her nose was running, and Jonati kept interrupting to wipe it. When the prince and princess were wed at last, Millie gave the baby back to Jonati and excused herself to return to her room.

She found her diary beneath her Bible on the bedside stand, and wondered once again if her aunt had indeed been reading it. She opened it to the pages she had written during Cousin Horace's visit two years before. Yes, she had written a great deal about her cousin's manservant John, and how he had refused freedom when it was offered to him. But perhaps Horace Jr. had spoken of it to his stepmother. *Lord, help me not to jump to conclusions,* Millie prayed. She flipped through the pages she had written during

A Sneak and a Thief

Cousin Horace's visit, her prayers for his little daughter Elsie, her hopes and prayers for her friends and family in Pleasant Plains, and her struggles in telling her friends about the abolition issues that day at their Bible study. Millie traced the lines of her writing with her finger. She had been so angry with Lu and Helen that the nib of her pen had torn the paper. *How can I write that I am a slave owner? How can I put that in this book, after everything I have said, after every speech I have given?*

"Have I not commanded you?" Millie's nervous flipping of pages had ended with the page on which she had copied the Scripture verse God had given her before she started on her journey. *"Be strong and courageous. Do not be terrified; do not be discouraged, for the Lord your God will be with you wherever you go."*

Be strong and courageous. . . . It does take courage to act on what you believe. I purchased Laylie to keep her safe. But they are going to take Luke away in three days. There must be something more I can do!

When Millie inquired after her uncle, Miss Worth informed her that he had retired to his sanctuary after the peppermint ordeal. Millie paused before she knocked on the door of the library. She had seen her uncle lose his temper when Aunt Wealthy had disagreed with him on the matter of little Elsie. Millie was sure she never wanted to hear him thunder at her in such a manner, but she was even more sure that something had to be done on Luke's behalf. She sent a quick prayer toward heaven and then rapped on the large wooden door. It opened under her hand. Uncle Horace looked up from the papers on his desk and motioned for her to come in. Millie was too nervous to settle into the cushions of the chair he indicated, but she balanced on its edge.

She had never seen her uncle smile, but surely his face looked grimmer than she had seen it before. *Has Enna's trouble affected him that much?* The baby girl was Uncle Horace's favorite, very much like Isabel in looks and temperament.

"Enna seemed quite recovered," said Millie.

"I believe she is," Uncle Horace agreed. "And she has learned a valuable lesson as well. What is troubling you? Is it that incident with the borrowed slave?"

"You are very perceptive," Millie said. "I have come to ask that you purchase Luke, or at least let him remain here. The slaves and their overseer will be returning to Meadshead in three days, and I do not think he is fit to travel. I have reason to believe that the overseer does not like him. I am afraid he may do him more harm on the way."

"Borse is a harsh man," Uncle Dinsmore said. "But I cannot believe he would willingly damage or destroy valuable property. I believe Luke will be treated as he deserves."

"And if he is not?" asked Millie.

"It is not my concern," Uncle Horace said. "It is the business of my father-in-law." He turned back to his papers, as if to dismiss her.

Millie folded her hands in her lap and waited quietly. She had seen that look on her uncle's face before, at Aunt Wealthy's house.

"You have something else to discuss?" he asked, looking up.

"I am not finished discussing Luke," Millie said. "Forgive my forthrightness, but I must do what I think is right. And I think you should, too."

"You believe I should do what *you* think is right? Yes, your family tends to be of that opinion."

"That's not what I meant," Millie said, flushing slightly. "I don't believe you are being honest with yourself, Uncle.

I have been with you for weeks now and I have seen the way you treat your people. I know you believe you treat your slaves well."

"I believe I practice common human decency," he said.

"You allow them gardens, and they are better dressed than the slaves from Meadshead. Why is that?"

Uncle Horace did not answer, so Millie continued. "I do not believe you would willingly send that young man back to Meadshead, knowing that he may be beaten to death."

"I don't know that he will be beaten to death," responded Uncle Horace.

"But you don't know that he will not be, either. Have you seen what Borse did to him?" she asked.

Uncle Horace's shoulders drooped the slightest bit. "I will write to my father-in-law, asking to purchase him. Will that satisfy you?"

"I would be very grateful," Millie said honestly. "But I will not be satisfied while slavery exists. It is wrong."

Uncle Horace stood up and started to pace the floor. "You are the most hard-headed young woman I have ever met. But your opinions and reasoning are persuasive. Perhaps you can help me with a matter that is troubling my household? I started to speak to you about it once before, but we were interrupted by Charles." He stood and started to pace, his hands locked behind his back. "I should have told her sooner, that much is clear now. I only wanted to protect her from anything that could cause her pain, do you understand?"

"I'm afraid I do not," Millie said.

"It's that . . ." He glanced at Millie. "Pardon me. What I meant to say is that somehow Isabel has found out about Horace Jr.'s child." Millie remembered her aunt's thick-as-cobwebs perfume, and she put her hand over her mouth, remembering the words she had penned: *"My heart breaks for Cousin Horace and the baby daughter he has never seen. And for little Elsie, whose mother died so soon after her birth . . . ." Aunt Isabel has been reading my diary. I'm sure of it!*

"It's terrible, I know," Uncle Horace said, mistaking Millie's reaction. "I would have done anything to keep it from her."

When did Aunt Isabel read my diary? It could not have been before I reached Roselands, since I carried it in my bag. But as soon as I unpacked, I put it on the table by my bed, just as I do at home. Scenes flashed through Millie's mind: Uncle Horace pacing the floor of the library, troubled; Isabel sitting at the breakfast table with her husband, a rumpled smile on her face. *Surely she knew even then.* Isabel must have read about little Elsie soon after they arrived—probably the very next morning, when Millie and Uncle Horace had taken their horseback ride to the sea.

"Isabel won't tell me where she heard about the child," Uncle Horace said. "She is protecting a friend, no doubt. But she is horrified. Can you understand? To join a member of the codfish aristocracy with the Dinsmore name! What was my son thinking to marry a girl from a family that made its money by common trade?"

"That he was in love," Millie said. "And that he wanted to be with her the rest of his life. I don't understand how I can help you with this, Uncle. You know my feelings about it."

"That is precisely how you can help. Horace is my son, but no part Isabel's. As his father, I must bear his indiscretion." He ran his hand through his hair. "Surely, because she loves me, Isabel will learn to accept the fact of what my son has done." *Is there a hint of doubt in his voice?* Millie wondered.

Uncle Horace went on. "Isabel does not have one friend who will not look down on her because of this. Not one. Be a friend to her, Millie. Help her understand that the actions of her stepson cannot tarnish who and what she is."

"I will do my best, Uncle Horace," Millie said slowly.

"I am relieved that Isabel will have someone in whom she can confide during my absence." He sat down once more.

"You are leaving us?" asked Millie with surprise.

"Just for a week. I must travel to Charleston for a meeting with my solicitor. I leave tonight, and should be gone no more than five days. I'm sure Isabel cannot bear this burden alone any longer than that."

In the hallway once more, Millie paused to settle her thoughts. *How could Uncle Horace possibly be worried that the actions or deeds of another would besmirch Isabel? Were her own misdeeds truly invisible to him?* Millie had a sudden vision of a spider with all of Roselands in her web. Millie herself was no more than a gnat, wrapped and ready to serve her aunt's needs. "That is nonsense, Millie Keith!" Millie said the words out loud, causing a kitchen slave who was passing to jump, glance at her sideways, and scurry away down the hall. *God brought me to Roselands, not Isabel Dinsmore. And God told me to be strong and courageous, didn't He?* Tendrils of doubt touched Millie's heart. *Maybe it wasn't God speaking to me that day at all. Maybe I just remembered that Scripture as I stood on the bridge. I do have many Scriptures memorized, after all. What made Joshua 1:9 so special?* Millie shook her head. It was so easy to stand firm at home. If she ever felt confused or doubted, she simply talked to Mamma or Pappa, or Claudina, or Reverend Lord . . . . She had not only her family, but also a whole church to encourage her. But the vision of the gnat came back, struggling and alone, and Millie shivered.

Millie's Faithful Heart

Well, if she had been alone when the sun rose this morning, she certainly was not alone anymore. She had one person—Laylie—that she was responsible for. Millie thought of the young girl standing quietly, waiting to be told what to do; peeking over Millie's shoulder, eager for words she was forbidden to read; crying for her brother. Laylie's sweet, innocent little face was enough to break the hardest heart. Surely God had sent Millie here for Laylie. And even Aunt Isabel, with all her plotting, had worked into His plan by offering the child to Millie. Now all Millie had to do was bide her time and play the piano at a few parties, and she would win Laylie's freedom.

It occurred to Millie that she knew nothing of where Laylie slept, what or when she ate, or what she had to wear. Isabel would be the wrong person to ask. Mrs. Brown, the housekeeper, was given charge of the house slaves.

Millie found Mrs. Brown in the kitchen, supervising the preparation of the evening meal. Phoebe, the cook, was stirring a thick gravy on the stovetop, while two younger women peeled potatoes.

"I have some questions regarding Laylie," Millie said.

"Is she not performing her duties?" Mrs. Brown asked, a worried look on her face.

"It's not that," Millie said quickly. "It's . . . I have purchased the child from Isabel, and I wish to know more about her."

"You bought yourself some trouble," Phoebe said.

Mrs. Brown's forehead wrinkled. "I was not aware that Isabel sold Meadshead slaves," she said, "but I can't say that I'm sorry. That child is too delicate for the fields."

Phoebe snorted, "Delicate as a 'gator, and just as sweet."

"Where does she sleep?" Millie asked.

"On a mat behind the stove in the kitchen. She puts her bedding away in the closet off the kitchen each morning," Mrs. Brown said, almost apologetically. "I wasn't expecting any new slaves, you see. Our house servants' quarters are full, and no one wanted to share a room with her."

"She wasn't sent here to work in the house?" Millie asked, outraged at the thought of the tiny girl working all day with the grown men and women in the fields.

Mrs. Brown shook her head. "I saw her in the wagon with the slaves who were sent up to help with the harvest and I asked if I could have her for the duration of their stay. I thought that she might be able to learn skills that would make her useful in the house at Meadshead."

"And she is a good worker, I'm sure," observed Millie.

"No, Miss Millie," said Mrs. Brown, looking truly worried now. "I wish that I could tell you that she is. But she is not."

"There's something more, isn't there?" Millie asked, searching Mrs. Brown's face.

"Other'n that child stealing and lying and who knows what all else?" Phoebe said. "No, not much."

CHAPTER

2

Just the Right Words

I can do everything through him who gives me strength.

PHILIPPIANS 4:13

tealing and lying? Surely not!" Millie shook her head. *But why not? What do I really know about the young girl?*

"Laylie might have stolen sugar lumps and biscuits," Mrs. Brown said.

"Isn't she allowed to have sugar or biscuits?" asked Millie.

"Of course she is allowed to have them," said Mrs. Brown, slightly outraged. "Mr. Dinsmore allows his house slaves sugar in their tea and a biscuit with their supper — but not the whole bowl of sugar and an entire pan of biscuits. Everyone else had to do without. Laylie has not been popular with the house slaves since that little episode, whoever was responsible."

Millie thought of Laylie's thin frame. *How could she have eaten an entire pan of biscuits?* "You are not sure Laylie took the food?" asked Millie.

"She took it," Phoebe said. "No one else did."

"She never admitted it," Mrs. Brown said.

"Borse would have had it out of her in no time," Phoebe said. "They don't allow that kind of nonsense from field slaves at Meadshead!" Phoebe's tone of voice made it clear that she did not believe that all slaves were created equal, and that Laylie, for one, had stepped out of her place.

"We are not at Meadshead, and that is quite enough!" Mrs. Brown said. Phoebe went back to her stew, muttering under her breath.

"And her clothing?" Millie asked. "She brought it with her?"

"She was wearing the shirt all Meadshead slave children wear," Mrs. Brown said. "One of the laundresses has a daughter just bigger than Laylie. Laylie is wearing her hand-me-downs."

"Thank you, Mrs. Brown," Millie said. "Could you have a cot put in my room for Laylie? I would like to have her close by me."

"Yes, Miss Millie." Mrs. Brown sounded relieved. "It is just as well someone is taking charge of her."

"You will regret it," Phoebe said to Millie. "Surely you will."

"I've heard what you did for Luke," Mrs. Brown said, "and I think it was wonderful."

"I didn't do anything, really," Millie said, suddenly embarrassed. "I simply asked Uncle Horace to send for someone to care for him."

Mrs. Brown pursed her lips. "That's more than most young ladies would have done. I have some soup left over from lunch if you would like to take it down to him. Something should be done about that Borse."

"Thank you," Millie said. "Just let me move Laylie's blanket to my room first."

"You shouldn't be doing that," Phoebe said disapprovingly. "White folk don't do that kind of work."

"I'm quite used to it," Millie replied. She didn't add that she intended to check the blanket carefully for lice and wash it if necessary before she moved it to her room. "Which closet will I find it in?"

"I'm going that way now," Phoebe said. "I'll direct you."

The blanket was neatly folded on top of a thin mat. It was new and clean, and Millie was sure Mrs. Brown had provided it for the child. She started to unfold it, and stopped. There was something wrapped in it — something square and hard, about the size of . . .

"Thank you, Phoebe," Millie said, tucking the bundle under her arm. She hurried up the stairs to her room and shut the door behind her before she unwrapped the blanket. Folded into the center was a beautifully illustrated copy of *Robin Hood*, a stub of a candle, and a box of matches. Millie flipped through the book, looking at the illustrations. Ru had the same book back at home. It had been one of his favorites when he was little. Millie was sure this book had been taken from Uncle Horace's library. And she was sure Arthur knew that Laylie had taken it. *"Thieves get whipped." That's what he said. So why hasn't he told?*

Laylie had obviously been looking at the pictures by candlelight, trying to figure out the story. Millie wrapped the book back up in the blanket and shoved the whole bundle under her bed before she went back to the kitchen.

"Field people don't need rich food," Phoebe grumbled as she pulled the soup kettle from the stovetop and wrapped the handle in a towel so that Millie could carry it without burning herself. "It'll make their stomachs sour, and make them forget their place. They'll be thinking they're as good as house slaves, and forgetting where they belong."

"Thank you for the soup," said Millie. She took the kettle of soup and walked across the garden and through the woods. *Laylie took a book from the library. That isn't stealing, is it? Yes, it is*, Millie reasoned with herself. *The book did not belong to her, and she knew she was not allowed in the library. But that doesn't mean she stole the food, does it?* Millie had a sinking feeling in her heart. Somehow she knew that Laylie had stolen the food. *Buying Laylie so that I can free her seemed like a good idea at the time, but I'm not wise enough to raise a child, and I have no idea how to keep her out of trouble. Mamma would know what to do, or Pappa, or Aunt Wealthy, but they aren't here.*

Millie's Faithful Heart

Millie walked through the footpaths of the quarters, past the whipping post to the cabin where Luke slept with the other slaves from Meadshead. Everyone else was in the fields.

"Laylie?" Millie whispered, pushing the door open. "Are you here?"

Old Rachel was sitting in a rocking chair by a small fire in the middle of the floor. Millie was surprised to see a Bible open on her lap.

"Afternoon, Miss Millie," the old woman said.

"I don't remember a chair in this cabin," Millie said.

"You want to sit in it?" the old woman asked, starting to rise. "I had it brought over so I could sit by this child all night. My bones are too old for the pallets."

"No," Millie said quickly. "Please don't get up." Luke was sleeping soundly, and Laylie was nowhere to be seen.

"Are you a Christian?" Millie asked. "I see that you are reading a Bible."

Old Rachel laughed. "I am, bless the Lord, and I knowed you was too, the minute I laid eyes on you. The Spirit testified to my spirit, as the Good Book says. You put that soup right down here, and let's have a talk. This young man is sleeping sound, and won't wake for some time. I have something to say to you."

Millie set the kettle down by the fire and, not seeing a chair, set herself down beside it. The door opened and Laylie peeked in.

"Luke still sleeping?" Laylie asked.

"Out!" Old Rachel said, pointing at the door. "Nothing you can do here! If I needed you, I would'a called you." The door shut, and Millie could hear children's voices calling Laylie away.

"Heard a rumor," the old woman said, kicking her heels to set the chair rocking, "that you bought that Laylie child."

Millie could feel her face starting to flush. "I . . . I . . . don't believe in slavery." It felt good to say it out loud. "It was kind of an accident. I mean . . . I don't even know if I have done the right thing. If I don't believe in owning slaves, maybe I shouldn't have. Maybe I won't buy her. I can still say no." Millie's voice faded away as she realized Old Rachel was looking at her.

"Don't believe in slavery," Old Rachel shook her head. "Now that's something."

"Surely *you* don't believe in slavery?" Millie said.

"I don't?" Old Rachel sounded surprised. "You seem a little young to be telling an old lady what she believes."

"Forgive me," Millie said. "I didn't mean to be rude."

"Well, now. I think I can forgive," Old Rachel said, her brown eyes twinkling. "That's what my Master would want me to do, isn't it? I can even show you a thing or two, if you are willing to learn from an old slave."

"Yes," Millie said. "I am willing."

Old Rachel flipped through the pages of her Bible. " 'Were you a slave when you were called? Don't let it trouble you—although if you can gain your freedom, do so. For he who was a slave when he was called by the Lord is the Lord's freedman. Similarly, he who was a free man when he was called is Christ's slave. You were bought at a price; do not become slaves of men.' "

"*You* were bought with a price, Miss Millie," Old Rachel said. "So was I. Jesus gave His life to pay for us and set us free. There ain't one thing man can do to take that away. But these children, Luke and Laylie, they're still in bondage. It's not the overseer with his whip that they have to fear. We're all of us goin' to die one day. It's dyin' before they know the Lord that they need to fear—dyin' before they know a price has been paid to set 'em free for all eternity. Now, you can change your mind about that girl. Go home and tell folks you never did own a slave," Old Rachel said. "Or you can pay the price for her and get her free from that evil place for a time. Maybe long enough to tell her about Jesus." She rocked a while and then looked up. "So, what are you gonna do?"

"I'm going to do what Jesus would do," Millie said. "I'm going to try, anyway."

"Good," Old Rachel said. "That's good. Because that child may end up costing you more than you think."

Luke stirred, and Old Rachel stood up to reach for a log for the fire. "This one, now, this one's mine. I've been prayin' over this child night and day. He's not stayin' at Roselands, and may not have much time on this earth once he goes back to Meadshead."

Luke groaned and turned over. "I need to take care of him now, and I don't think he wants a young lady present."

"Yes, I'll go," said Millie, turning to leave. She stopped with her hand on the door. "Thank you, Miss Rachel," she said, smiling softly.

"I have a Scripture for you," Old Rachel said, stirring the fire. " 'I can do everything through him who gives me strength.' That's Philippians 4:13 if you want to look it up. That Scripture is true for an old slave woman, and it's true for a young lady like you, too. Not some things, Miss Millie. That's not his promise. He says you can do *all* things."

Tears sprang to Millie's eyes. Her Aunt Isabel may have been reading her diary, but God was reading her heart. And He had sent someone to speak just the words Millie needed to hear. Millie knew how Mary and Joseph must have felt when Anna, the eighty-four-year-old temple prophetess, spoke God's words of encouragement to them about their baby, Jesus. Millie had just read that story in her Bible in the second chapter of Luke.

"Thank you, Miss Rachel," Millie said again. "You have no idea how much I needed to hear that. May I come talk to you tomorrow?"

"I'm not making any promises," Rachel said. "The Lord just might call me home tonight. Who knows? Now scoot."

Millie was halfway through the woods when she caught a flash of movement out of the corner of her eye and stopped. Laylie was at the bottom of a small hollow standing straddle-legged on a log over a ditch. A boy was facing her. He couldn't have been older than Laylie, or he would have been working in the fields already, but he was twice as tall as the young girl. Each child was holding a broomstick in front of them . . . like . . . like a quarterstaff. They were acting out a scene from a picture in the *Robin Hood* book — Robin facing Little John on a footbridge.

"You will not pass!" Laylie said loudly.

The boy apparently had not looked at the pictures. He swung his longer arms around his head, and before Laylie could reach him, he clobbered her alongside the head. Laylie disappeared into the briars with a cry.

"Don't hit Laylie," a little girl yelled, picking up a dirt clod and hurling it at the boy. The children took up the hue and cry, flinging mud and rocks at the boy.

"Laylie!" Millie called. The children scattered and quickly disappeared. Laylie scrambled out of the bushes, brushing leaves from her apron.

"Yes, miss?" Laylie said fearfully.

Millie's Faithful Heart

"Are you hurt?" asked Millie with concern.

"No, miss." Her ear was bleeding where the quarterstaff had clipped it.

Millie pulled her handkerchief out of her pocket and pressed it to the wound. "Hold this," Millie said, as she felt a cough coming on. She turned away from the young girl until the coughing fit passed.

"That sounds bad, miss. Are you dying? Miss Jayla had a cough like that and she died." It was the longest speech Millie could remember Laylie ever making.

"No, I'm not dying. Not imminently, at any rate," Millie said. "I need you to come with me now. There is something I want to talk to you about."

They stopped in the kitchen and Millie asked for a pinch of black pepper powder from Phoebe. The cook looked disapprovingly at Millie's clean handkerchief pressed to Laylie's ear, but handed over the pepper anyway.

When they reached Millie's room, Laylie looked in dismay at the cot that had been placed in the room.

"You will be sleeping in here from now on," Millie explained as she rinsed the cut with water from the basin and dried it with a clean edge of her handkerchief. "Now be still while I sprinkle pepper on it. It will stop the blood flow."

Laylie squeezed her eyes shut.

"It's not going to hurt," Millie assured her. She sprinkled the pepper on the cut and waited for the small ooze of blood to cease.

"How did you learn that, miss?" asked Laylie.

"You learn many things on the frontier," Millie laughed. "Especially if you have little brothers like mine. And that brings me to this." She pulled the blankets and mat from under her bed and unwrapped the book, candle stub, and matches.

"Those are not mine, miss," Laylie said quickly.

"That is correct," Millie said. "They do not belong to you. This book belongs to Uncle Horace. You took it from his library. And the candle and matches came from the kitchen cupboard. And none of them are yours."

"I've never seen them before," said Laylie with her eyes opened wide. "Honest, miss," Laylie added with emphasis.

"Really?" Millie opened the book to the illustration of Robin and Little John on the footbridge, and stopped. There was a caption beneath the picture. "You shall not pass," it read.

No wonder Laylie showed little interest in learning to read. She already knew how! And her eyes weren't following my finger across the page. She was reading over my shoulder!

"Laylie, who taught you to read?" Millie asked.

"No one," Laylie said. "Slaves don't know how to read."

"That is nonsense and you know it. Old Rachel was reading her Bible just now as she cared for your brother. Have you finished reading this book yet?" she asked, holding up *Robin Hood*.

"No, miss." Laylie's voice was almost a whisper.

"My uncle said that I could borrow any books I like from his library and keep them in my room. I will borrow this book and allow you to read it, since you already know how. But you must promise not to lie to me. And stop calling me 'miss' when we are alone. Call me 'Millie.' Can you do that?"

Laylie looked longingly from Millie to the book. "Yes, mi . . . Millie."

"Now we will see how good you are at telling the truth." Millie held out the book. "Would you like to hold it while we talk?"

Laylie nodded and took the book.

Millie's Faithful Heart

"How did you learn to read?" Millie asked.

"Andros taught me," replied Laylie.

"Andros?" inquired Millie, puzzled.

Laylie looked at Millie uncertainly, then shrugged. "He lived in the swamp when I was a little girl, eating snakes and possums. Luke caught rabbits to pay him to teach me to read. Andros had three books, but he up and disappeared one day." Laylie leaned forward and lowered her voice. "Folk said he got dragged to hell by sixteen witches, kicking and screaming the whole way."

"You don't believe that, do you?" Millie asked with surprise.

Laylie shook her head. "If he did, he took his books with him, an' his cook pot, too, 'cause I went and looked. Nothin' left in that hut but snake skins and possum bones."

"Did you steal sugar lumps and biscuits from the kitchen?" asked Millie.

Laylie's eyes dropped to the book, and then went back to Millie's face.

Now, if this were Cyril, Millie thought, *he would be considering how much I already knew. He'd make sure he didn't confess too much. He might not exactly lie, but he certainly would not tell me the whole truth.*

Laylie swallowed hard before she spoke. "I stole them," she said.

Millie's heart dropped. She had been hoping that Laylie had not stolen the food.

"Did you eat them or hide them?" Millie asked, never taking her eyes off Laylie's face.

"Neither," Laylie said. "I took them to my Merry Men."

The little children in the quarters! Of course! Millie almost laughed. *That's why they follow Laylie around. She brings them sugar and biscuits and who knows what else from the house, and tells them stories about Robin Hood!*

~

That night, Millie read her Bible as Laylie brushed out her hair. The young girl read over her shoulder, but Millie read aloud anyway, liking the sound of the words.

As Millie opened her diary, Laylie stretched out on her stomach reading *Robin Hood*, so absorbed in the story that Millie could see the emotions moving across her face. *What can I write to God that I won't mind Aunt Isabel reading?* Millie asked herself, smiling. *Lord*, she wrote, *I don't know how anyone can miss the fact that You exist. The very nature of the world around us testifies to You. How empty life would be without You. Tonight I can only pray the words of Psalm 8:*

'O Lord, our Lord, how majestic is your name in all the earth! You have set your glory above the heavens. From the lips of children and infants you have ordained praise because of your enemies, to silence the foe and the avenger. When I consider your heavens, the work of your fingers, the moon and the stars, which you have set in place . . .'

Millie finished writing out her psalm, and waited until Laylie reached the end of her chapter before she said it was time for sleep. Laylie handed over her book, and Millie damped the light.

"I talk to God before I go to sleep each night," Millie said. "Would you like to talk to Him, too?"

"Why?" Laylie asked.

"Well . . . He is my best friend. I can tell Him anything. Don't you talk to your best friend?" said Millie.

Millie's Faithful Heart

"Luke's my best friend. He says only fools talk at night when they could be sleeping."

"Luke probably says that because he is tired," Millie said. "But God never gets tired, and He is always listening for your voice. He wants to hear what you have to say."

"Then he can talk to me first," Laylie said logically. There was a long moment of silence. Millie wasn't sure whether she should say anything, or what she would say if she did.

"Guess he's not talking," Laylie said matter-of-factly. "He must be tired like Luke after all." She pulled her pillow over her head.

Millie knelt by her bed and bowed her head. *I know You are listening, Lord Jesus,* she prayed silently. *And it is a good thing, too, because I don't have any idea how to tell Laylie about You. Or how to keep her out of trouble for that matter. Lord . . .* Millie groped through her mind for the right words to express just what she needed. She was sure the words would have flowed like sweet water from her Mamma or from Aunt Wealthy, but she could find only one word that expressed her need: *"Help!"*

She crawled into her bed and pulled the blankets up to her chin, but she lay awake for a long time, staring into the darkness. She was sharing a room with a pint-sized Robin Hood. Millie was quite sure she was not numbered among the Merry Men. *Does that make me the Sheriff of Nottingham? A fat abbot?* She was glad Laylie had left her quarterstaff in the woods.

CHAPTER

3

True Freedom

*It is for freedom that Christ
has set us free.*

GALATIANS 5:1

*A*unt Isabel did not eat breakfast until ten o'clock, but Millie, mindful of her promise to her uncle, waited for her. When the breakfast bell rang at last, Millie entered the dining room to find her aunt in a rare good mood, seated at the head of a table adorned with lovely hothouse flowers. The Dinsmore children were up earlier than usual and sat at the table with their mother. Jonati, their nursemaid, stood quietly against the wall, keeping an eye on them all.

"Good morning," said Aunt Isabel. "I trust you slept well?"

"I did, thank you," Millie said, taking a seat. Once she had managed to fall asleep, Millie had slept restfully enough. "Those are lovely flowers, Aunt Isabel."

Louise and Lora giggled.

"Do you think so?" Isabel said, turning the vase. "They came this morning, addressed to you. It seems you have a secret admirer. I knew you had made a conquest at the party!"

Millie felt a blush creep up her cheek. She had met several young men at Aunt Isabel's party, but had been very careful not to flirt.

"Charles Landreth sent them!" Louise said. "Mamma is sure of it! And that's not all! He sent chocolates!" Millie's blush grew deeper. Aunt Isabel had her heart set on creating a connection between the Dinsmores and the Landreths. Charles was heir to a large fortune, so Isabel was sure Millie would jump at the chance to win him.

"Louise!" Isabel laughed. "You must work on your dramatic timing. It is very important to romance!"

Millie's Faithful Heart

"There is no drama here," Millie said firmly. "I think Charles Landreth is a fine young man, but I am not looking for a romance."

"Well if you don't want the chocolates, I do!" Arthur said, reaching for the box.

"Arthur! Mind your manners," snapped Isabel. "You stop that this instant or leave the table." Arthur hiccupped and gulped his way to a stop, but the rest of the family was paying no attention to his theatrics.

"Why would he want to marry *her*?" Louise asked. "I think she's too thin."

"Mother is planning on marrying you off before you can leave Roselands," Adelaide explained in a whisper, "so you can stay with us forever."

Millie had to bite her lip to keep from saying that it would be horrible to stay with them forever.

"That's not why," Lora said. "Charles Landreth is a catch! And he has a lot of money."

"Hush, Adelaide, Lora," Isabel said firmly. "Stop licking your spoon, Arthur, and for heaven's sake, stop that annoying hiccupping! Jonati! Do something about this!" She waved at baby Enna, who had her chubby little finger up her nose. The nursemaid picked the child up.

"Now, why are you actin' like dat? Do you want your mamma to be ashamed of you?" Jonati said.

"It's no wonder we don't have you at breakfast with us often," Isabel said to her brood. "You would think children of your breeding would have better manners."

"Perhaps their manners would develop if they sat at the table more often with you and Uncle Horace," Millie suggested. "They could learn by your example."

"Now are you an expert on child raising?" Aunt Isabel said. "I don't suppose you would like to set an example for them every single morning?"

Millie looked at the faces around the table. Adelaide's seemed hopeful; Louise's and Arthur's merely interested — in the same way they would be over a bug at the table; Lora was occupied with her jam and bread. *This could be a solution to part of my problem. If I can take Laylie to the nursery with me, I can keep her out of trouble.*

"I would not mind having breakfast with my cousins in the nursery if you would allow it, Aunt Isabel," Millie replied. "It might ease my homesickness for my own brothers and sisters."

"Very well," Isabel shrugged. "I am rarely awake by breakfast anyway."

Millie bowed her head and prayed before starting her breakfast. Uncle Horace enforced a strict silence while Millie prayed, but in his absence the children continued their eating and prattle, unconcerned.

They finished their breakfast with Jonati's keen eye over the children. Isabel directed that the flowers be delivered to Millie's room, and the box of chocolates as well.

Millie asked to be excused, and went back to her room to check on Laylie. Her own brothers and sisters had chores they attended to, but Mamma and Pappa always made sure they had plenty of time to play as well. If Laylie spent two hours a day in the quarters with her friends, then she would be out from under foot, and it would give Millie time to spend with Aunt Isabel or her cousins. *Surely Laylie won't try to run away. There has to be something I can give her to do that will keep her out of Phoebe's way. What usually occupies Adah and Zillah's hours?* By the time Millie reached her room she had a plan.

Millie's Faithful Heart

"I have something for your Merry Men," Millie said, holding out the box of chocolates. "But you can't take it to them until after the signal for the field hands to go back to work after their meal."

Laylie took the box and sniffed it. "What is it?" she asked.

"It's candy," Millie explained. Laylie still looked blank. "Like sugar lumps, only better." Millie opened the box and took out a piece of chocolate. "Here. Taste it."

Laylie popped it in her mouth and chewed slowly. The wrinkles cleared from her brow, to be replaced by a look of amazement.

"I thought you'd like that," Millie said, closing the box. "But your friends will have to share. I don't think there are enough pieces here for each child to have a whole one."

"They'll share," Laylie said firmly, and Millie was sure they would. "But why can't I take it to them now?"

"We have other things we need to do. Do you know how to sew?" Millie asked.

"I sewed a shirt last year at Meadshead," Laylie said proudly.

"Good." Millie opened her wardrobe. "Do you remember when I told you the story of Cyril and his pet skunk?" Laylie nodded. "Well," said Millie, "God used that to provide us with plenty of material to make clothes for you. Let's see what color suits you best."

Laylie immediately reached for the green silk with French lace.

"Not that one," Millie said. "That one is from a very special friend. Choose any other."

Laylie quickly passed over Damaris's dark, somber dresses. It seemed her taste ran more to Lu's extravagant styles. She was delighted with one pink silk, holding it up and twirling around for all the world to see, like Zillah would have done. Millie smiled. "We'll start with that one," said Millie. "I will cut it down for you, and you can help. But I want to see the quality of your needlework before you try any seams. You will work on pantalets and petticoats first."

Millie set to work taking the seams out of the pink dress, while Laylie worked on the pantalets. Millie was thankful for all of the hours she had spent taking in dresses for her own little sisters. It was not a difficult task if you understood the fabric and the cut. There was plenty of material in the dress. If she altered the style just a bit, she would have enough left over to make a matching bonnet. It would look stunning against Laylie's dark cream complexion.

It was immediately apparent that unless Laylie's skills with a needle exceeded her ability to pull stitches, Millie was going to be doing much of the work herself.

When Mrs. Brown appeared at mid-morning with the mail, Laylie was still hard at work over her first seam. After handing Millie her mail, the housekeeper looked with approval at the work Laylie was doing. "That is a good way to keep her hands busy," she said as she left. Millie was pleased to find a letter from her mother, and another from Rhoda Jane.

"Are those from your family back home?" Laylie asked, as Millie unfolded the letter from her mother.

"Yes," Millie said. "One is from my Mamma and the other from a friend."

Laylie bit the thread, not bothering to use the scissors. "Are there slaves there—where they live?"

"No, Indiana is a free state," Millie answered. "Sometimes slaves travel there with their owners for a visit, but people who live in Indiana do not own slaves."

Millie's Faithful Heart

"How long did it take that letter to get here?" Laylie asked.

"A month," Millie said, checking the date at the top of the letter. "It came by boat and stage, I'm sure."

"How long would it take if your mamma had just handed it to someone who was walking?" Laylie asked.

"A few months at least," Millie replied. "It would have taken so long, I would be on my way home by then! Do you want to hear what she says?"

"Yes," Laylie said with a hint of excitement in her voice.

My Dearest Daughter,

Your Pappa and I pray that this letter finds you in better health and strong in the Lord. I was thankful to read in your last letter that your cough is not so severe in the milder climate. God is so good to provide this opportunity for you. I am confident that you are bringing honor to your mother and father by all of your decisions.

Here Millie glanced at Laylie. *I hope Mamma would be proud. I'm sure if anyone would understand my decision to buy Laylie, it would be Mamma.* Millie read on.

Fan has lost her two front teeth, and her whistle has gone with them. Cyril and Don immediately invented a whistle language and tormented the poor thing by whistling their messages back and forth. Gordon came to her rescue, making her a wooden-slide-whistle. The house now sounds like an aviary, though the world outside is locked in ice.

Millie finished the letter, chuckling over the news of her brothers and sisters and friends, then tucked the letter in

close to her heart. Laylie finished ripping the seams in silence, and Millie was just as glad. She missed her family so much it hurt. She had to remind herself that it was now late November; last year at this time, she had been lying in bed with a comforter pulled up to her chin and Mamma acting as her nurse. Her lungs were better here, even with the wet weather, and she felt stronger every day.

As Millie was about to read the letter from Rhoda Jane, they were interrupted by the sound of a distant shot. Laylie looked up. Millie had been disturbed by the shots in her first days at Roselands, until Uncle Horace explained that they were simply signals for the slaves. This one released them for their meal; in an hour and a half they would be summoned back to work by another shot.

"We'll wait until the workers go back to the fields," Millie said. "Then we will carry a meal down to Luke. If we finish these seams, you may spend the rest of the afternoon with your friends."

Laylie went to work with a vengeance, picking at the tiny stitches so quickly that she pricked her fingers half the time.

"Try not to bleed on the fabric," Millie said, as Laylie put a finger in her mouth to suck off a bright red bead of blood.

Just then there was a knock on the door, and Arthur entered without waiting to be invited in. From the way Laylie's expression changed, it was not the first time she had encountered Arthur. She looked as if she had just swallowed a cup of cod liver oil.

"Hello, Cousin Millie," he said, his eyes going around the room. They landed on the box of chocolates, and he edged toward them. "I was wondering what you were going to do with these?"

"I have already given them away," Millie said. "To Laylie." Arthur picked up the box and opened it.

"Arthur," Millie said sharply. "Put that box down. It doesn't belong to you. If you take something that belongs to someone else, it is stealing."

"*I'm* not a thief," he said, giving Laylie a significant look. "Nobody would whip me. And you can't steal from slaves. You just take what you want, because they don't own anything." He chose a chocolate. Millie set her sewing down and quickly crossed the room. She took the chocolate from his hand just before it reached his mouth.

"I said no!" Millie insisted, her eyes widening at Arthur's arrogance.

"I'm going to tell Mother," Arthur sneered.

"Good. I am proud that you will confess to your mother. Stealing is a sin," replied Millie firmly.

Arthur's eyes narrowed, but his look was for Laylie, who had not said a word.

"I don't mean about the chocolate. I mean about the. . ."

"Book?" Millie said. She suddenly wondered if all of the sugar lumps Laylie had taken had found their way to her Merry Men. *Has Arthur been blackmailing Laylie into stealing sugar for him?* From the sour look on his face, Millie was sure of it. "Your father has given me permission to read any book in his library, and to take them to my room," Millie said, holding up the book. "Would you like me to read you a chapter of *Robin Hood* this afternoon?"

"No," Arthur said sullenly. "I hate that story. And slaves shouldn't have chocolates." He stomped from the room, slamming the door behind him. Laylie flung the pantaloons against the back of the door, then went and kicked them where they fell.

"Laylie," Millie said, trying to keep her voice as calm as Mamma's would have been. "Pick those up and finish ripping the seam, or we won't be able to see Luke this afternoon."

An hour later Millie carried the box of chocolates to the kitchen. They stopped long enough to ask Phoebe for bread and butter and a piece of cold meat.

"You bring my kettle back this time," Phoebe said, addressing Laylie. "Don't leave it down there."

"Yes, ma'am," Laylie said, even though it had been Millie who had borrowed it.

As soon as they entered the woods, little faces began peering out from behind trees. The children were obviously waiting for their leader. Laylie ignored them, keeping her eyes straight ahead until they reached the cabin that Luke was in. Old Rachel was sitting in the rocker in the same place, but this time her Bible wasn't on her knee. Luke was awake and they had obviously been talking. The fever had left him weak, but he was able to lean on his elbows.

"Hey, Luke," Laylie said. "I brought you something." She shoved the chocolates at him. "But you can't have them all."

"You speakin' to me again?" Luke said. "Last I heard you hated me."

"That's enough of that kind of talk," said Old Rachel. "I have all you children together here just one time, and I'm too old to waste my breath. I'm going to tell you the truth and I don't know how many times you're going to hear it, so listen good."

Laylie took a step back.

"Sit down, Laylie," Luke said. "I want to hear what she has to say." Laylie eyed Old Rachel with caution and then sat down slowly.

Millie's Faithful Heart

"I know you want freedom," Old Rachel said. "I have wanted it myself, many a time, with a wanting worse than hunger, worse than thirst. I knew the taste and feel of it when I was your age. I was born a free woman in Africa."

"Did white men catch you?" Laylie asked.

"Child, sin doesn't live under just one kind of skin. I was captured and sold by men with skins as black as mine. I was purchased and beaten by men whose skins were white. You see this?" She waved at Luke's back. "That don't come from black or white. That comes from sin in the hearts of evil men. I know—I got scars just like them on my back." She was silent for a moment as she rubbed grease into Luke's wounds. "I've been offered my freedom since then. I said no. I wanted to stay right here."

"Why?" Luke asked. "I would give anything to be free."

"You remember that Jesus I been tellin' you about?" Old Rachel asked, looking from Luke to Laylie. The two of them exchanged a glance. "I know you do," said Old Rachel. "Well, Jesus faced a choice one day. He could let evil men beat Him and nail Him to a cross. Or He could walk away. He had the power to do it. He chose to stay and die—to save me and to save you from the evil one. When I was offered my freedom, I thought about the choice He had made. I thought about the children here who needed to hear about Him. And I stayed."

"He's gonna save us from the masters?" Laylie asked. "They are evil. I hate them."

"Then you just get over that right now," Old Rachel said. "Hate is a sin, and I told you, sin is not particular about skin color. You can't tell me you never met a bad slave."

"Robson," Luke said, wincing from the memory of his beating. "He helps Borse."

"And maybe you have met some good white folk now," said Old Rachel, looking at Millie. Millie certainly hoped that it was true, but neither Luke nor Laylie met her eye. "You have a choice," continued Old Rachel, "you can be given to evil like Borse and Robson, or you can be given to good, like me and Miss Millie. It don't have anything to do with the color of your skin. It has to do with your heart. It's either washed clean of sin, or it's not. If it's not, then you will never be free, no matter how far you run."

"You mean becoming a Christian, like you were talking about?" asked Luke.

"That's right," said Old Rachel.

"What does it mean, exactly?" Luke sat up. Laylie edged closer to him.

"It means accepting the fact that you are a sinner," Old Rachel said, "and because of that, you can't ever get to heaven. The only way is through Jesus—by gettin' credit for His pure heart. 'Cause Jesus was the only one that never did nothin' wrong. So God—who's His Father—let Him go up on that cross and die for all our sins—yours, mine, and everybody else's, too. All you gotta do is accept that free gift. Then, one day, you'll be with Him in heaven, where there won't be no more hurtin' or cryin' or pain, 'cause in heaven, lambs will even lay down with lions. So are you children ready to give your lives over to Jesus?"

Luke put his arm around Laylie and pulled her close. He sat there with his brow scrunched, deep in thought, for a minute. "No," he said at last. "I want my life to be my own."

Old Rachel shook her head. "Your life won't ever be your own. If you don't belong to Jesus, then you are a slave of sin. No matter how far you run."

"I got to think about it," Luke said.

Millie's Faithful Heart

"You do that," Old Rachel said. "We got until sundown tonight, and then I got to go home. My pass is only good until then."

They talked for another hour before Millie realized that she had to go. Aunt Isabel's company would be arriving soon.

"Laylie," Millie said. "I expect you to come back up to the big house when Miss Rachel leaves."

"I'll see she does," Old Rachel said.

Millie said her goodbyes and hurried through the woods. *I would give anything to stay and pray and talk to Luke and Laylie about Jesus, but I made a deal. The price I have to pay to keep Laylie is so insignificant compared to the price Old Rachel paid to be here to speak to them.*

Millie did her best to be entertaining all evening. This was the second party Isabel had hosted since Millie's arrival, and Isabel took full advantage of her guest, insisting that Millie wear the finest gown possible, and seating her between a bewhiskered old gentleman and Charles Landreth for dinner.

After the meal, the company retired to the parlor, where Millie played the show tunes Mrs. Lightcap had taught her and the songs she had learned on the canal boats. Charles Landreth leaned on the piano and Otis Lochneer sang along.

Isabel's guest lists tended to include every eligible young person in the neighborhood, as well as those older people who had power, influence, or almost as much money as the Dinsmores themselves. The young ladies gravitated to Charles Landreth — as if his good looks and fortune had a magnetic force — leaving the less wealthy young men standing in the corners. Millie decided that the young man was quite a snob, and that if he had been so foolish as to send her flowers, he could take them right back. It was well past midnight when she crept into her bed exhausted. Old Rachel had been as good as her word; Laylie was asleep on the cot.

CHAPTER

4

Speaking Up

"Hear me, you who know what is right,
you people who have my law in
your hearts: Do not fear the
reproach of men or be
terrified by their
insults."

ISAIAH 51:7

Speaking Up

*D*awn was a gray promise when Millie woke. "Laylie?" She knew by the stillness of the room that she was alone. *Where has she gone so early?* Millie pulled her clothes on quickly, not bothering to take off her nightcap. She grabbed a cloak, slipped her feet into her shoes, and hurried down the servants' stairs and out the kitchen door.

A fine, steady November rain was falling, cold as needles of ice. Millie put her hood up as she hurried through the woods toward the slaves' quarters. The not-quite light of morning was darker still under the trees, and she wished she had brought a lantern. She stumbled more than once on roots or rocks in the path. The light was better by the time she reached the slaves' quarters — and made even brighter by lanterns on poles.

Three wagons were drawn up in the center of the quarters. One was already full of men, sitting in the cold rain. Another group was standing, watched over by a man with a whip and gun. They were called forward one by one to stand still while a blacksmith fastened a heavy iron fetter around the right ankle of each. When the fetter was in place, they moved down the line, and the end of a chain was fed through the hoop on the side of the iron anklet, linking them all together. A group of women were huddled together under the eye of another overseer. Two older girls had hold of Laylie. One held her arms, while the other was trying to pull the shoes from Laylie's feet. A woman had already taken the girl's apron and was wearing it herself; another had the cloak Laylie had worn when she went riding or walking with Millie. Millie was sure the young girl had not given either of them up any more readily than she was giving up her shoes.

Millie ran toward them. "Put her down!" Laylie was instantly dropped in the mud. She stood up and aimed a kick at the larger of her assailants, and a punch at the other, but the older girl skipped aside.

"Who is in charge here?" Millie demanded.

"That would be me." The man supervising the blacksmith stepped forward. "Mr. Ronald Borse, head overseer of Meadshead."

"Why are you shackling these men?" asked Millie.

"Master's orders. We're going back home, and they're always in irons when we move them. Saves chasing them if they run." Borse spat a reddish-brown stream of tobacco juice. "And who is it that asks?"

"Mildred Keith. And I will thank you to remember your manners in the presence of ladies, sir!"

"Ladies?" Borse looked from Millie to the group of women and laughed.

"Boss?" The blacksmith looked up. "That there's Master Dinsmore's niece. I seen her when Ajax brings out the horses for her to ride."

Borse took a step back. "Ladies don't belong down here. You run on home, now."

"Not until I have seen to Laylie's brother. I doubt that he is in any condition to travel."

"We put that one in the wagon already. Condition or no condition, he's going today," Borse said. "It's my job to bring them all back, dead or alive."

"Which wagon?" asked Millie.

Borse indicated with his chin. Millie stepped on the spoke of the wheel and pulled herself up to look into the wagon bed.

Speaking Up

Luke was sitting on the bare boards, shirtless in the icy rain. Laylie scrambled past Millie and into the wagon. "I'm here, Luke," she said, sinking down beside him.

"You can't go up there, miss," Borse said, as Millie started to follow.

"Of course I can," Millie said. "I am quite strong and can manage very well, thank you."

"You mistake my meaning," he said. "These are Meadshead wagons. You keep off them."

"This is Dinsmore land." Millie had struggled up into the high wagon. She took off her cloak and laid it over Luke's shoulders. "Shall I summon my uncle and explain how you feel about your wagons?"

"I could have sworn he left on business yesterday and won't be back this week," Borse said slyly.

Millie bit her lip. She had forgotten that Uncle Horace had a meeting with his solicitor. "Then as long as you are on Dinsmore land, I speak for my uncle," she said firmly. The men with whips looked to Borse, who shrugged and turned his back on Millie.

"Luke," she said, kneeling beside him and speaking in a voice low enough that only the three could hear. "Are you . . . able to travel?" She felt foolish as soon as the words were out of her mouth.

"I'm fine, miss, just fine," he said. "You stay here with Miss Millie, Laylie, and do what I said."

"I won't stay!" Laylie's whisper was fierce. "Don't you dare. . . ," she glanced at Millie, "go without me!"

"Laylie, girl," Luke grinned. "I won't never go nowhere without you could I help it."

"Promise, Luke." Luke reached for Laylie's hand. He pressed it against his chest.

Millie's Faithful Heart

"You feel that old heart thumpin'?" he asked.

Laylie nodded.

"It's sayin' Lay-lee, Lay-lee. You think I could forget you one minute with that racket going on in there? As long as my heart keeps thumpin', as long as wild geese fly . . ."

"As long as the North Star shines," Laylie finished his sentence.

Luke nodded. "The promise I made you stands."

As long as the North Star shines? They are talking about running away! Millie realized. *Luke is promising to come back for his sister!*

"Luke, I . . ." Millie started, groping for words. *Of course they wouldn't trust me to help. What can I do, anyway?* "I'll take care of her," said Millie.

"Better get out of there, miss." Millie jumped at Borse's words. *Did he hear what Luke said, too? Did he understand?* The shackled men started loading into the wagon before Millie could answer. Millie gave up her place, but Laylie clung to her brother.

The wagons started forward, the wheels picking up the red Carolina mud, flinging it in the air and spattering the women who followed in the wagon ruts on foot. Borse rode in front of the lead wagon on a big chestnut horse.

Millie walked along with the women as they started down the road toward town. She followed them up the long drive, giving Laylie as much time with her brother as possible. When they reached the end of the drive, Millie called, "Laylie, come on down now."

There was no answer from the young girl. "Laylie, do you hear me? Driver, I need to get her out!" Laylie wasn't the only one ignoring her. The team plodded on, the driver apparently deaf to Millie's voice. *Do they think they can just drive off with the child?*

Speaking Up

Millie picked up her skirts and ran to the head of the team, grabbing the harness and pulling the horses' noses down hard. "I said stop!"

"What is going on here?" Borse turned and reined in his horse to stop beside Millie.

"I want Laylie off that wagon. She has to go back to the house with me."

"That girl's not going anywhere," Borse said. "I told you, I bring them all back."

"Not this one. Mrs. Dinsmore sold her to me."

"That right?" Borse tipped his hat back on his head with the butt of his whip. "Funny, Mrs. Dinsmore didn't say a word to me about it. You have the papers?"

"Papers?"

"You buy a horse, you get papers that say you own it. You buy a slave, it's the same thing. I'm not letting her go without papers. Let me tell you a secret." He leaned forward. "That little gal is going to end up the same place as her brother—six feet deep. And it's me that's going to put her there."

"Let me tell you something that is not a secret, sir!" Millie said. "My uncle would not be amused to hear you calling his favorite niece a liar! That child was sold to me by Isabel Dinsmore, papers or no papers. Now turn over my slave!"

"Mr. Dinsmore will peg your hide to the barn, boss," the driver said. "Even if he has to follow you to do it. He don't allow nobody to disrespect his ladies."

Borse turned deep red and the sides of his neck seemed to swell. He jumped from his horse, threw the reins to the driver, and climbed into the wagon. Slaves cowered away from him as he made his way to the front where Laylie sat beside her brother. Laylie screamed as he lifted her by one arm. "Shut up," he said, slapping her face.

"Let her go!" Millie yelled, trying to get her foot up on the spoke of the wagon wheel so she could pull herself into the wagon. Her head was just high enough to see Luke start up to help his sister. Borse hit him one blow with his fist, and Luke collapsed in a heap on the wagon floor. The thick mud on the sole of Millie's shoe slipped on the spoke, and she lost her grip on the wagon. She jumped to pull herself up again, but before she could even get her foot on the spoke, Borse held Laylie out at arm's length.

"You want her? Here!" He tossed the young girl. Her body flew through the air, like one of Fan's dolls tossed from her tree house, arms and legs akimbo. She landed in a mud-filled ditch.

"You beast!" Millie yelled at Borse. She ran after Laylie, slogging through the knee-deep mud to pick her up. The young girl didn't seem to be hurt badly.

"You won't get those papers," Borse said. "I'll have her next year, or the year after. You'll see."

Millie wrapped her arms around Laylie, turning her away from Borse's hate.

"Shhhh, Laylie," Millie said, rocking her, even though Laylie wasn't crying. "It'll be all right." They stood in the mud together, watching the wagons until they disappeared.

"Let's get back to the house," Millie said at last.

Soaked skirts and petticoats were almost impossible to walk in. Millie led Laylie to the kitchen entrance. She couldn't imagine coming in the front door of Roselands looking like this. They went up the servants' stairs to Millie's room where Millie started stripping the clothes off of Laylie first.

Speaking Up

"May I come in?" asked Mrs. Brown from the door. She looked from Millie to Laylie and shook her head. "They're gone then?"

"Yes," said Millie.

"Good riddance to bad rubbish," Mrs. Brown said, stoking the fire and putting on another log to warm the room. She turned and started helping Millie with Laylie's petticoats, which were completely soaked with mud.

"I will find something for her to wear," the housekeeper said. "You had better hurry and dress, Millie. It is the Sabbath, and Mrs. Dinsmore has decided to make an appearance at church."

The Sabbath? I've lost all track of the days! "I can't possibly go and leave Laylie right now," said Millie.

Mrs. Brown wrapped a blanket around Laylie and settled her by the fire. "This child is safe for now. But the farther away Borse is, and the happier Mrs. Dinsmore stays, the safer she will be. Do you understand?"

Millie looked at the shivering little form. "How much time do I have to get ready?"

"Good girl," Mrs. Brown said. "You have half an hour, at the most. Mrs. Dinsmore does not like to be late. I'll take care of Laylie and this mess. I wouldn't mention any of this to Mrs. Dinsmore, if I were you." She gathered Laylie's clothes under one arm and put the other around the young girl, and ushered her toward the door.

"Mrs. Brown?" Millie called after her. The woman stopped. "Thank you," said Millie.

Millie struggled out of her clothes after they had left, leaving them in a sodden pile on the floor. She poured water from the pitcher into the porcelain bowl and tested it with her finger. Ice was warmer. Cupping it in her hands she splashed it on her face and neck, then rubbed them dry with a towel.

The dressmaker had delivered her black silk the day before, and Millie hurried into it. She brushed her hair and swept it up in a French twist, thankful that her nightcap had protected it from the rain and mud. The reflection that stared back at her from the mirror certainly looked like a composed young lady. It was a good thing mirrors could not see the inside of people, because Millie felt as if she were still standing in the cold puddle of mud, furious at Borse and the whole world.

"Oh, here you are!" Aunt Isabel exclaimed when Millie appeared at the breakfast table. "I was just wondering. You look quite stylish. I won't be ashamed to exhibit you as a relative of the Dinsmores!" Two carriages were brought, as Isabel insisted that the younger children ride in a separate one with Jonati, and off they went.

The church was lovely wood and stained glass, with arched ceilings and quiet corners. Millie felt at home at once, surprised at the feeling of peace that surrounded her. Aunt Isabel stayed in the vestibule, talking to friends and acquaintances, but Millie walked into the sanctuary and seated herself. If God had a parlor where He sat with friends, Millie was sure it would feel just like this — peaceful and somehow deeply happy. No, happy was not the right word. Joyful. Like the tingle of excitement you have just before you hear the good news of a baby's birth, or of a loved one coming home at last.

Millie bowed her head. *Thank You, thank You, thank You, Lord, for rescuing Laylie this morning! Watch over Luke, and let them be together again.* Millie wondered, *Did Luke give his life to Jesus yesterday? I had no chance to ask Old Rachel.* She lost herself in prayer for the brother and sister, for her own family, and for the Dinsmores.

"Oh, there you are!" said Isabel.

Millie was truly surprised to look up and find the seats full around her. "This isn't the Dinsmore pew," said her aunt. "We will have to move."

Millie stood up to follow her aunt to the front of the church. Jonati and a few nursemaids and personal slaves sat along the back wall. Old Rachel was there beside Jonati, her Bible in her lap. Her face was glowing, and Millie knew that the old woman felt the same peace she did. The rear rows of the church were full of common people — like people Millie would have seen at a service in Pleasant Plains. As she moved forward with Isabel, the incidence of fur muffs, feathers, and jewels increased. Isabel marched boldly to the front pew. It had a little box around it, almost like the one Millie had sat in at the theater in Philadelphia.

"This is the Dinsmore pew," Isabel announced, opening the little gate and ushering Millie inside. After settling herself on the pew, Isabel produced a small mirror and checked her hair. "There he is," she whispered. Millie thought from her tone of voice that she was speaking of God Himself, or at the very least the minister. Realizing that was not likely to be the case, she started to turn, but Isabel elbowed her. "Don't look back!" She held up the small mirror again, pretending to straighten her hat, but turning it so that Millie could see.

Charles Landreth had taken a seat two pews behind them. Otis was with him. Millie sighed and opened her Bible.

"He's staring at you," Isabel said. "How delightful!"

Millie focused on the sermon. Reverend Ogilvie's message from the book of 1 Timothy on the requirements for church leaders was very good, although it caused some squirming. Millie was only distracted once or twice by a warm feeling on her neck. *Is Charles Landreth staring at me? Surely not. I am sitting directly between him and Reverend Ogilvie, after all. What is he doing here anyhow? He claimed that he would run screaming from church. Or did he say that I would run screaming if I met his aunt?* Isabel lifted the mirror again, but Millie resisted the urge to look.

After the close of the service, friends and neighbors gathered for friendly chats in the vestibule. Many people stopped to welcome Isabel home and inquire about her recent trip, and to make Millie's acquaintance. Old Rachel was standing quietly behind a pleasant-looking woman of about fifty. Millie smiled at them as she made her way through the crowd. She desperately wanted to ask Old Rachel how her talk with Luke had gone, but the slaves who stood on the outskirts of the crowd took no part in the socializing. They stood as silent as furniture, holding the coats and hats of their masters, or here and there carrying a baby or a child.

"Why, Millie Keith!" the woman standing in front of Old Rachel said, taking Millie's hand warmly. "My name is Eugenia Travilla. I am an old friend of your mother's, and I would have known you anywhere, even before you showed your dimples. You have Marcia's lovely eyes. And her heart for Jesus, too, from what I hear."

"I can think of no greater compliment," Millie said. "Mother has spoken highly of you."

"You must come visit at your first opportunity," Mrs. Travilla said. "I want to hear all about Marcia and that rash young man she married!"

Rash young man? Pappa? Millie felt her dimples peeking out again. *I would really like to hear Mrs. Travilla's stories!*

"How are you today, Mrs. Travilla?" a deep voice asked. "And Miss Keith?" Millie turned to find Charles Landreth standing at her side.

"Charles!" Mrs. Travilla cried. "I haven't seen you in church since . . . "

"Since the unfortunate incident with Calvin? Yes," he said.

"I was going to say since you were thirteen years old, but now that you mention it, that was the last time you attended church. I always wondered what happened to the poor fellow."

"He suffocated, I believe," he said, winking at Mrs. Travilla. "At least that is the gentlemanly thing to say."

Mrs. Travilla nodded knowingly. "He was very small, Charles. But under the circumstances it would not have mattered how large he was, I'm afraid."

"How horrible!" Millie said. "Your friend died in church?"

"He was quite dead when we managed to roll Mrs. Jorgenson off of him," said Charles.

"Her fainting spells were practically earth-shaking events," Mrs. Travilla explained. "And precipitated as that one was . . . "

"Oh, dear," Millie said. "I am so sorry."

"Don't be," Charles said, patting her shoulder. "He had led a good life and was quite old, I understand—for a mouse."

His words took a moment to sink in. Millie looked from Mrs. Travilla to Charles. Suddenly Mrs. Travilla laughed. "Forgive me, Millie. You haven't changed a bit, Charles Landreth!"

"But I have!" Charles protested. "I have a gold watch in my pocket instead of a pet mouse."

"Well, you should bring those pockets to church more often, no matter what you have in them," said Mrs. Travilla.

A sour-faced woman in a loose-fitting black dress stepped forward. "Levity is hardly appropriate here," she said. The severe cut of the woman's dress did nothing to hide the fact that she was all odd angles and points from her elbows to her nose. Even her eyes were sharp. Millie almost wanted to take a step back when she met that disapproving gaze.

Charles sighed. "Aunt Clara, may I present Millie Keith? Millie, my aunt, Clara Landreth."

"Pleased to meet you," Millie said, smiling and offering her hand.

The woman took Millie's hand in one of hers. If Millie had had her eyes closed, she could almost have imagined a rough, bony chicken's claw gripping her fingers.

"We must be running," interrupted Aunt Isabel, who had appeared on Millie's other side. Taking Millie's arm, she started to the door. "Come along, Millie!" They had almost reached the door when Isabel turned back. "Oh dear! I have forgotten my umbrella."

"You weren't carrying an umbrella, Aunt Isabel," Millie said.

"Nonsense. Charles, would you be a dear and hand Millie into the carriage? I'll be right along."

Charles bowed and then followed Millie down the path toward the waiting carriages.

"I was surprised to see you here this morning," Millie said. "I thought you fled everything religious."

"I hope I am open-minded. I thought, after our discussions, that you might have seen something in church that I have not," Charles said.

Millie stopped. "I apologize," she said. "I didn't mean my comment to be rude. I have had the most horrible morning imaginable up until the time I walked into the church." She started walking down the path again. "I suppose I should thank you for the flowers."

"I didn't send any flowers," Charles said. "Should I?"

"You didn't?" Millie frowned. "I mean no, of course you shouldn't. I would rather no one did."

"I see," Charles said, stopping to help her over a patch of mud.

"Did you?" Millie asked as they reached the carriage. "See anything you have not seen in church before, I mean?"

"Most definitely." Charles offered her his hand as she stepped into the carriage. He shut the door behind her and then leaned in the window. "I have never seen mud behind such lovely ears before. Good day, Miss Keith!"

Millie's hand flew to her ear, and came away with a crust of red mud. Her instant outrage dissolved into laughter as she imagined what Aunt Isabel would think if she ever learned *why* Charles Landreth had been staring at the back of Millie's head through the whole service.

Millie was particularly attentive to her aunt on the way home. "Aunt Isabel, I was wondering . . . . Since we have made a deal on Laylie, when will I get the papers?"

"Papers?" Aunt Isabel's eyes narrowed. "My word isn't good enough for you?"

"Of course it is," Millie said quickly. "But someday, when I leave . . . "

"Oh, that's simply ages away," Aunt Isabel said. "I'll worry about it tomorrow. I have invited Regina—she was the one in the blue—and Charles and Otis over for the afternoon."

Millie's Faithful Heart

Millie washed behind her ears thoroughly as soon as she arrived at Roselands. Laylie was nowhere in sight, but as it was Mrs. Brown's afternoon off, Millie could only trust that the child was with the housekeeper. Millie had a cold dinner with Aunt Isabel and then excused herself. Jonati had taken the children to the nursery, as far from their mother as possible, as Aunt Isabel needed a nap before the company arrived.

After the meal, Millie sought out Mrs. Brown's rooms.

"Mrs. Brown, it's Millie Keith," she called, knocking.

"Come in," Mrs. Brown said as she opened the door. Millie stepped into a pleasant apartment with a roaring fire. It was very simply furnished, with a small bed, a table, and two stuffed chairs. Mrs. Brown had been perusing a book in front of the fire in one chair; Laylie was curled up asleep in the other.

"I wanted to thank you for your help this morning," Millie said. *Can I trust her enough to tell her that Laylie might try to run away?* Something inside whispered, *"Be cautious."* "I'm worried about Laylie," Millie said. "Her brother was very dear to her. I don't feel comfortable leaving her alone."

"Don't worry a bit," Mrs. Brown said. "When she is not with you, I will watch over her."

CHAPTER

5

Steal Away to Jesus

*He is wooing you from the jaws of
distress to a spacious place
free from restrictions.*

JOB 36:16

*W*hen Millie went downstairs again, she found Charles standing in the hall, his hat in his hand. "Miss Keith!" he said, as if surprised to see her.

"Just one moment," Millie said, walking over to the mirror. She stretched her lips to examine her teeth, and turned one way and then the other to check behind her ears, then turned with a smile. "Mr. Landreth!"

"I see that vanity is not one of your vices," he said with a laugh.

"My concern is wholly for my aunt," Millie said. "It has been my experience that your presence is a kind of jinx, and I wish to spare her humiliation."

"I am sure no one else noticed the mud," he said. "If they had, I was fully prepared to rush outside and apply some to my own ears. We would have created a new fashion craze."

Millie was quite sure he would have done it. She found herself laughing up at him, and realized that she had not laughed in days. "Why are you wandering the halls? I did not hear the bell ring."

"I am here so often that it would wear out the servants' shoes answering the door. In the interest of saving leather, Horace has instructed me to come and go at will. I was looking for him just now."

"Uncle Horace was called away to visit his solicitor in Charleston," Millie explained. "He will return in a few days."

"I wondered why he was not in church. Isabel rarely appears without him. He is such a stunning accessory—tall, dark, and handsome, with a dash of silver at his temples. He sets her off to good advantage, don't you think?"

"I doubt Uncle Horace thinks of it that way. And . . . " Millie fumbled for words.

"Ah-ha!" Charles said, as they started toward the parlor. "You can't disagree about Isabel, can you? You see her more clearly than Horace does."

"She is my aunt," Millie said, "and that is uncomfortably close to gossip."

They had reached their destination, and Otis leapt to his feet as they entered and offered Millie a chair. They spent a pleasant afternoon talking and playing parlor games. By the blush that came and went on his cherubic cheeks whenever she spoke with him, or even looked his way, Millie was soon sure that it had been Otis who sent her the flowers and candy. *Lord, should I speak to him about it? If I do, what should I say?* She had no desire to play with the young man's heart, or give him encouragement when her own heart would never be his. The option of not speaking about it at all was taken away by Otis himself, who followed her across the room away from the others.

"Did you like the flowers I sent?" he blurted, and then covered his mouth with plump, jeweled fingers. "Oh! I wasn't going to say that. I promised myself I wasn't. But everyone knows I can't keep a secret." Here he flushed quite pink. "I grew them for you."

"The flowers were lovely," Millie said. "But you could not possibly have grown them for me. You have known me less than a week. I was not even at Roselands when you planted them and cared for them."

"I was thinking of you nonetheless," Otis said. "I simply did not know your name."

"That seems improbable," Millie replied. "What do you know of me even now? We have just met."

"I know you have the face and form of an angel. I would give all my worldly fortune just to be near you. My heart . . . "

"Mr. Lockneer," Millie said. "Let me be perfectly clear. I do not want your flowers, your chocolates, your fortune, or your heart."

"That . . . that is clear," Otis stuttered. "Very clear."

"Mr. Lockneer," Millie said, trying to soften the blow. "I am sure you are a marvelous young man. But I am not here seeking romance. I am only here for the winter, and then I will be returning to my home."

"Then . . . I have no chance?" He looked like a cocker spaniel puppy that had just been put out in the cold.

"I have given my heart . . . " Millie was going to say "to Jesus," but before the words could leave her lips, Otis collapsed onto the couch.

"You belong to another," he groaned. "It always turns out this way for me. He's a rugged frontiersman, isn't he?"

"Isn't who?" asked Charles Landreth, who had wandered over.

"Millie's fiancé," Otis said. "He's a frontiersman. I feel unwell. I am afraid I have to go."

Otis's departure broke up the party, and Millie was left with the evening to herself. She found Laylie at work in the kitchen, and took the girl to her room. There she spent the evening writing letters to her family, while Laylie lost herself in her book. The young girl occasionally stared off into space and Millie wondered if she were thinking about her brother. Laylie had not mentioned his name all day, and when Millie asked if she would like to pray for him, Laylie just shrugged. So Millie tucked the young girl in before she knelt and prayed aloud for her own family and for Luke. Laylie pretended not to listen, but after the lights were out, she tossed and turned on her bed.

"Millie?" she asked at last from the darkness. "Starting from Roselands, how far is north?"

Over the next few days, life at Roselands arranged itself in a busy routine. Millie rose early for her Bible study. It wasn't a private devotion time, as she read aloud to Laylie and then discussed what she read. Millie had discovered that the young girl loved the sound of the Psalms, but Millie decided to read through the book of Matthew so Laylie would know the whole story of Jesus. Millie had spent some time thinking about how her own parents had taught her about faith in the Lord. She could still remember the day when she knelt with her Pappa by the side of the bed and prayed for Jesus to take over her life. But it had seemed like she'd always known Him, and Bible reading had always been part of her daily life. Millie's parents had taught her that true faith was "lived out daily." She saw true faith in their godly example, and Millie wanted Laylie to see it in hers, too.

After Bible reading, Millie and Laylie had breakfast with the Dinsmore children in the nursery. Millie was able to give Laylie a plate, but Laylie could not sit at the same table as the Dinsmores, so she had her breakfast sitting on the floor. At ten, Millie had tea with Aunt Isabel, who was just rising. Millie tried to be true to her promise to Uncle Horace to be a strength and solace to her aunt, but Aunt Isabel never mentioned Elsie Dinsmore. In fact, she seemed to need no strength or solace Millie could provide. After tea, Millie would go for a walk or ride with Laylie, taking her sketchbook along. The bird-watching in the gardens was marvelous — Millie was able to see several new species on the first day. After the noon meal, when the Dinsmore children were released from their lessons, Laylie was allowed to play in the woods with the children from the quarters while Millie spent time with her cousins.

When the sun went down, the world changed. The children were sent to the nursery with Jonati or Miss Worth. Millie put on a pretty new gown, and Aunt Isabel's hairdresser appeared. Hot irons were applied, ribbons arranged, and Aunt Isabel came to inspect the result. It was after sundown that Isabel seemed to come alive. She sparkled like a diamond when she entertained, looking fresh and beautiful no matter how late she stayed up. It was, Millie decided, a bit of a Cinderella story in which Isabel became a princess when the sun went down, but spent her days lying about only slightly more active than a pumpkin.

⁓

"I hope you are up to visiting today," Aunt Isabel said one afternoon. "I have already ordered Ajax to bring the carriage around. We will visit that horrible Mrs. Landreth first. If we don't, I'm sure she will come calling on me, and I know she considers me a mission field. I'm sure she thinks of me as a worldly-minded woman, a kind of heathen in fact."

"Why would you think that?" Millie asked.

Millie's Faithful Heart

"She has told me so," Aunt Isabel said, slipping her hand into her glove. "She prays daily for my conversion."

Isabel complained about the hardness of the seats in the carriage as Ajax cracked the whip over the horses. "There!" she exclaimed as it bounced over a small stone. "I'm sure I will have bruises. Be a dear, Millie, and rub my head. The thought of Mrs. Landreth gives me a throbbing headache."

"Then why do you visit her, Aunt Isabel," Millie asked, "if she is not fond of you, and you are not fond of her?"

"She doesn't know that I am not fond of her," Isabel said. "She is from a good family, and as I have told you before, the Landreths are quite wealthy. It would be wrong to snub them. This is simply part of the price we pay for our position in the community. I am surprised that your own mother has neglected your education in these things, Millie."

Isabel was silent for so long that Millie was sure she had fallen asleep, but an hour later when the carriage turned onto a poplar-lined drive, she sat up and said, "Oh, here we are!"

"The grounds are beautiful," Millie said, looking out over the well-kept lawns. "And the house as well."

"Skin deep, as some would say," Isabel sniffed. "But things will change around here when it belongs to Charles."

They were shown into the drawing room by a sad-faced slave, and told that Mrs. Landreth would be on her way shortly. The room was spacious but dreary, and very plainly furnished. Millie couldn't help but feel that even wilted flowers in a vase would have improved the aspect of the room. A respectable number of dead ancestors looked down sternly from paintings hung on every wall. Whether it was the company or location they found distasteful, Millie could not tell.

"A happy group, are they not?" Charles said, entering the room. "Grandaunt Beatrice actually smiled once. She was almost disinherited."

"You see what an excess of pious living can do," said Isabel, shuddering.

There was one spot of life in the room—a blazing fire—and above it a very fine painting of the countryside. Millie was drawn toward the warmth and the color, like a moth is drawn to a light.

"What a beautiful painting!" Millie said, examining it more closely.

"Yes," said Isabel, walking over to stand by her side. "It's the one handsome thing in the house, and she is forever after her husband to sell it."

"Do tell her you like it," Charles said. "I love it when people tell her that."

At that moment, Mrs. Landreth entered the room. The ill-fitting black dress the woman had worn on Sunday could be described as "happy," compared to the somber way she dressed at home.

"Good day, Mrs. Landreth," Millie said.

"Miss Keith," she said. She bowed her head ever so slightly, but she did not smile. Her face was ready to take its solemn place on the wall of ancestors, glaring disapprovingly down through eternity. She rang a small silver bell, and her sad-faced slave appeared with a tea tray and cups. Isabel and Mrs. Landreth exchanged views on the weather as the tea was served.

"Do you like the paintings?" Mrs. Landreth asked at last, turning to Millie.

Millie's Faithful Heart

"I admire the one over the fireplace very much," Millie said. "Such a lovely sunny landscape pulls at your soul. It makes you wish you could just step into it."

"Does it?" Mrs. Landreth sniffed. "I believe my husband committed a grave sin in purchasing it and hanging it there. It makes one discontent with one's lot."

"Thinking of heaven makes me discontent with my lot here," Millie said. "But it gives me something to look forward to. Just as that painting lets me look forward to spring."

"It is a frivolity," Mrs. Landreth said in a flat voice. "The Bible tells us to be content with food and clothing. We ought not indulge ourselves in anything more. That is why my clothes are plain and there are no frivolous decorations in my home. The money is better spent on charity."

Millie looked at Isabel, but her aunt seemed quite content to let Millie carry the conversation. Charles was no more help.

"I quite agree that we should give liberally to charity," Millie said. "But surely the God who created yellow daisies, blue robin's eggs, and peacock plumes would not mind if we brightened our homes or our clothing with color."

"Peacocks?" Mrs. Landreth sat up straighter.

Millie was unsure what she had said wrong, but was very sure she had committed an offense. "Yes. You must admit they are beautiful . . . "

"Are you suggesting, young woman, that I adorn myself as a bird?" asked Mrs. Landreth.

"Peacocks are lovely," Charles said, entering the conversation at last. "All of those . . . feathers."

"You know I consider the wearing of feathers vanity, Charles. Do you agree, Miss Keith?"

70

"Yes," Millie said in some confusion. "I mean no. God created beauty, don't you think?"

"I will suffice myself with inner beauty," Mrs. Landreth said, examining Millie closely. "Though I see that is not enough for some."

"Are you complimenting my looks, or criticizing my character?" Millie asked. Isabel's eyebrows went up a hair. Mrs. Landreth looked as if her tea had gone down the wrong way. Charles raised his teacup in a salute to Millie.

"Forgive me," Millie said quickly. "I sometimes speak before I think."

"I will pray for you," Mrs. Landreth said sternly. "For a wicked tongue is a sinful thing."

"Well, that was profitable in every way!" Isabel exclaimed as she and Millie settled once more into the carriage. "I have never seen Mrs. Landreth so ruffled! But," she patted Millie's knee, "Charles was certainly amused. You must let her be a warning to you, Millie. This is the result of too much religion, and the very reason I avoid it like the plague."

"It has been my experience, Aunt Isabel, that true religion—loving God with all your heart, mind, and soul, and others as yourself—produces just the opposite of this somber life," Millie said. "Think of every good thing you know—blue sky, babies' smiles, chocolate—God created all of these things. How could He be pleased with such grimness in the face of His gifts?"

Isabel yawned. "Pardon me, did you say something? My mind simply does not work in religious ways. I think that is why I have retained my youthful looks. I refuse to think of such things. Now we are on our way to Ion, and that shall be a more pleasant experience for both of us, though I can't help but feel that Mrs. Travilla compares me unfavorably with Horace's first wife."

"Surely not," Millie began.

"I am not given to fancies," Isabel said. "I assure you it is so."

They rode on in silence until they arrived at the Travilla plantation. Millie was immediately taken with Ion. The grounds were extensive, beautiful, and well cared-for. The house, a fine old mansion, was handsomely furnished. There were rare and costly pieces of art and paintings scattered throughout the rooms. Songbirds in cages added music to the atmosphere.

Mrs. Travilla was delighted to see them. "Thank you, Harold," she said to the servant who showed them in. "Ah, welcome, Millie dear. You looked like your mother walking through that door just now," Mrs. Travilla said, taking Millie's hands.

Mrs. Travilla had many questions for Millie about her family, but after a few minutes, Aunt Isabel began to squirm in her seat and made her impatience to leave apparent. It was plain to Millie that Aunt Isabel was not interested in hearing about her husband's relatives in Indiana, despite Mrs. Travilla's obvious interest. Nevertheless, for Millie it was a wonderful visit. Mrs. Travilla was blessed with the kind of hospitality that makes one feel not only comfortable but cherished, and the atmosphere in the Travilla home was so like that of her own home that it brought tears to Millie's eyes. Mrs. Travilla's kindness reminded Millie of her mother.

As they rose to leave, Mrs. Travilla said to Millie, "If Isabel can spare you, you must spend the day with me soon. It will quite restore my youth."

"I would be delighted," Millie said. "It will help me with my homesickness."

Uncle Horace returned to Roselands the next day, and to the great delight of the children, he refused all plans of going out. Instead, he gathered them around the fire in the parlor and read a book to them. Millie was relieved, having had too many late nights in the last week. Isabel left the children to their father, but Millie was pleased to see that she gave him a fond kiss before she went to her room.

"Stay a moment, Millie," said Uncle Horace when the children were sent to bed. "I received a reply on that matter you had me write Meadshead about."

Millie studied his face for a moment. "Mr. Breandan won't sell Luke?" she asked.

"It's worse than that, I'm afraid. I spoke to Borse. It is just as well that the young girl stayed here. Apparently her brother had a weak constitution. He never made it back to Meadshead. He succumbed to the same illness that took Laylie's mother."

"It wasn't an illness, Uncle. It was Borse."

Uncle Horace shook his head. "I cannot believe my father-in-law would allow such mismanagement of his property, or such inhumane behavior for that matter. They are a fine family, with a fine reputation. The young man did seem weak when I saw him. These things just happen sometimes."

Millie's Faithful Heart

He was silent for some minutes. "I will tell the girl," he said at last. "I would spare you that unpleasantness."

"No," Millie said. "I will tell her. It is better that it come from someone she knows."

Millie went straight to her room. In Pleasant Plains she had sat by the side of the dying and helped prepare the body for burial. But this was somehow more horrible. *Jesus,* she prayed, *I don't know what to say. Help me choose my words carefully.*

Laylie came into the room carrying an armload of fresh linen.

"Put those down and come sit with me," Millie said, patting the bed beside her.

Laylie obeyed with a frown. "Is something wrong?"

"Yes," Millie said. "Very wrong. Uncle Horace received word from Meadshead . . . "

"Luke's dead," Laylie said flatly.

Millie could only nod.

"He lied," the girl continued, as if Luke could have chosen another fate. "He said he was coming back for me."

"He didn't lie," Millie said. "He told you the truth. He would have come." Millie's eyes stung as she remembered Luke's words, "*As long as my heart keeps thumpin'.*"

"Luke wanted you to be free," Millie said, pulling the young girl into her arms, though it was like hugging a piece of wood. "I promise you I will not leave you here. You will be free, like Luke wanted. I'm not going to leave Roselands without you, Laylie. I promise. I'm going to take you with me to Indiana where you will be free."

"Is what Rachel said about heaven true? No more hurting or tears?" asked Laylie.

"Yes," Millie said.

Laylie sighed. "I lied to Rachel about Jesus people at Meadshead. The slaves there have a church. In the night, after everyone is supposed to be in bed, you hear them singing, 'steal away, steal away to Jesus,' and then some of them get out of their beds and they walk through the dark to the swamp. That's where they meet. Do you think Luke went before he died? Do you think he stole away to Jesus?"

"I hope so," Millie said. "He listened very carefully to what Miss Rachel had to say." Millie was silent for a moment, then she said, "Laylie . . . do you want to steal away to Jesus? You could pray to Him right now."

"No," Laylie said. "I want to be with Luke." Her sobs finally came, and Millie could only hold the young girl in her arms as she cried.

"Now, now," Millie whispered, stroking Laylie's head. "You just go ahead and cry as hard as you want."

CHAPTER

6

A Helping Hand

He who oppresses the poor shows contempt for their Maker, but whoever is kind to the needy honors God.

PROVERBS 14:31

A Helping Hand

*T*he weather turned fair the first week of December. Isabel planned excursions to various points of interest in the vicinity, and tea and dinner parties. In the daytime there were drives to town to shop for more finery. In the evening they drove to town for the purpose of attending concerts, lectures, and the opera and theater.

Otis, who had recovered from his heartbreak with astonishing speed, was almost always at Millie's side, and Charles just a laugh away. Millie wished that she could gather it all up—the lectures for Pappa, the concerts for Mamma, and the opera and theater for her brothers and sisters—and take it home to her family. She had to be content with writing about it in her journal, putting down every detail she could remember, for she was sure she would never see this type of life again.

Laylie was a different matter. The young girl went about her chores quietly, doing just what was expected of her. More than once Millie woke to find her at the window, gazing at the stars. Millie prayed as hard as she could, but still she was at a loss as to what to do for the child. She worked diligently on the pink dress and matching bonnet, and Laylie pricked her fingers less frequently, but they often worked in silence.

One afternoon, just as they were finishing their sewing, Millie looked out the window to see an Ion carriage rolling up the drive. Mrs. Brown came to the door with a note for Millie—an invitation for her to drive over to Ion and spend the day.

Millie's Faithful Heart

"I sent my carriage for you," wrote Mrs. Travilla, *"hoping it may not return empty. Uncle Eben is a careful driver. He will bring you over safely and carry you back when you feel that your visit must come to an end."*

"We are going to visit Ion," Millie told the young girl. She left a message for Isabel, who had not arisen, and soon they were rolling briskly along the road.

Mrs. Travilla received Millie in her boudoir. "Millie, dear! I have been looking forward to a visit from you. I hear you are quite the toast of the town. And who is this charming young lady?"

"This is Laylie," Millie said.

"Ah, yes. Rachel spoke of you, Laylie. She thinks you are a very bright young girl." At that moment, Old Rachel entered the room carrying a tray with a teapot and cups.

"Well," she said when she saw Laylie, "it appears I brought one cup too few."

"Yes," Mrs. Travilla said. "There will be four ladies at our party." She pulled a bell cord and a servant appeared. "Will you bring another cup?" Mrs. Travilla asked.

"Thank you," Old Rachel said, setting the tea service down as he disappeared. "That hall to the kitchen is getting longer every day. Either this house is growing, or my legs are shrinking." She settled herself into a stuffed chair.

Mrs. Travilla poured the tea, passing Rachel her cup first, then Laylie and Millie, serving herself last. Laylie looked at Millie as if she were unsure what to do. Mrs. Travilla saw the look and smiled. "Laylie, I believe you have met Rachel. But what you may not know is that she is my older sister." Laylie looked from one old woman to the next. "Oh, not my flesh-and-blood sister," Mrs. Travilla explained. "She was born in Africa, and I was born right here at Ion. But when I was a girl, and Rachel was not much older," here Old Rachel snorted, but Mrs. Travilla went on, "she led me to the Lord. On that day, we became sisters. And a sister is a wonderful thing to have."

"Couldn't wash my hair without you," Old Rachel agreed. "My arms are too stiff."

"And I couldn't have managed my home without you," Mrs. Travilla said. "My neck was too stiff."

"Well, well," Old Rachel said, smiling. "Between us we manage. We do manage." They smiled at each other, and Millie thought it was the kind of smile that took years to grow between two people—a smile that knew more than it could ever say.

"Laylie," Old Rachel said. "I was mighty sad to hear about your brother. Why don't you and me go walk and talk for a while. I had a brother, too, once upon a time."

Laylie looked to Millie, who nodded. Laylie stood to her feet, and Rachel started to rise, but made it only halfway.

"Let me help," Mrs. Travilla said, moving to her side. She grabbed her friend's arm and helped her up out of the chair.

"Hall's getting longer, chair's getting lower," Old Rachel said. "I guess that means I'm getting closer to heaven."

After they left, Millie told Mrs. Travilla all the news about her family and their life in Pleasant Plains. Mrs. Travilla wanted to hear everything, even the details of Marcia's work with the Ladies Society. The conversation continued until they caught sight of Old Rachel walking back across the lawn with Laylie.

"Don't give up on that child, Millie," Mrs. Travilla said. "Never give up."

Millie's Faithful Heart

Isabel decorated Roselands for the approaching Christmas holiday with candles, greenery, and fine and costly decorations in every room. The effect was enchanting, and Isabel held more parties and gatherings at her home in order to show it off. Millie played the piano for each gathering just as she had promised, and Isabel pronounced her "brilliant!" The guests seemed to agree. Roselands had become the place for all of the most stylish people to gather this season, and Millie was displayed as both an ornament and an entertainment.

The approaching holidays also meant more trips to the dressmaker. Uncle Horace provided Millie with a purse sufficient not only for the dresses, but to buy Christmas gifts as well, and offered to accompany her to town, where she could shop while he attended to his business. Millie was happy to accept. She spent a busy morning choosing gifts for her cousins, uncle, and aunt, and wandering the shops. Her final stop was at Mrs. Bissell's to pick up the dress she had ordered two weeks before. Millie was surprised to see Miz Opal, one of the delightful Christian women she had met on the steamboat during her journey to Roselands, in the window of the funeral parlor. Miz Opal's eccentric relations owned the parlor, of course, and she had invited Millie to stop by. But Millie had not expected to see her for a month at least. The thought of the Colonel and his stories, and Miz Opal's cousin Dearest who had married the funeral director and always dressed in widow's weeds, brought a smile to Millie's lips. She left her parcels with Mrs. Bissell and stepped next door.

"Millie Keith! I declare!" Miz Opal said as Millie stepped in the door. "I almost didn't recognize you. You look so much the young lady! Oh, won't you stay for tea?"

"I would love to," Millie said, glancing around. The room was set up as if for a funeral, with greenery and a coffin on a stand.

"Just a display," Miz Opal said, knocking on the coffin as they went past. She led Millie through a door into a tidy home behind the shop front. Here, Millie was introduced to a somber-looking man who was sitting bolt upright on the edge of his chair.

"Blessed Bliss," Miz Opal said, "this is Millie Keith. Millie is staying the winter with the Dinsmores. We met on the boat from Pittsburgh."

"The Dinsmores are an uncommonly healthy family," Blessed said mournfully. "I rarely get to see them."

"Thank goodness," Millie said, taking his hand. "I mean . . . pleased to meet you."

He nodded and his Adam's apple bobbed once. "Likewise, I'm sure."

"And you remember the Colonel?" said Miz Opal. The bespectacled man had risen when Millie entered. "Dee-lighted, dee-lighted!" the Colonel said, bowing. "I was just telling Blessed about the explosion of the steam engine of the *Best Friend* of Charleston . . . "

"Two dead," Mr. Bliss said.

"I believe Millie has heard that story," Miz Opal said, taking two teacups from the shelf and setting them on saucers.

"Not really!" The Colonel seemed shocked.

"I think I may have," Millie said. "Does it have something to do with cotton bales?"

"Say no more!" the Colonel cried. "I have not come to that part of the story yet!"

"Our young friend from the ship!" Dearest cried, entering the room.

"It was a boat," the Colonel corrected. "A ship is quite a different thing."

Dearest only clapped her hands. "I am delighted to see you! We have had no excitement around here, and no company either."

"Pull up some chairs," the Colonel said. "I will continue my tale. It is exciting enough to hear more than once, I'll wager."

"We were going to take our tea in the other room," Miz Opal said, handing Millie her cup and saucer. "Would you like a cup, Dearest?" Dearest would, and after finding herself one, led the way back into the front room. She drew the heavy, dark half-curtains across the windows so that they were shielded from the curious gaze of passers-by.

"It's the only parlor I have," Dearest explained, "so I make do. Wait!" Miz Opal had started to put her teacup down on the convenient table created by the coffin. Dearest raised the lid and reached inside to pull out a lace tablecloth. This she shook out and draped over the coffin to make a table. "Now put them down," Dearest said, pulling up three chairs. Miz Opal seemed to think nothing was amiss about these goings on, so Millie sat down.

"I apologize for the Colonel," Miz Opal said. "He does tell the same story over and over again."

"He's justifiably proud," Millie said. "Stacking bales of cotton on the flatcar behind the steam engine could save lives. It's a good thing he was there."

"I'm sure he is very proud. Unfortunately, he was visiting me in New York when that incident occurred. The Colonel has an overly active imagination."

"Oh," Millie said, blushing. "I didn't realize."

"He is a dear man," Dearest said. "But he longs for action, and whenever he reads an exciting account in the

newspaper . . . well, he simply imagines himself right into the story. It makes his life so much more exciting, you see. There is no harm in it."

"He yearns for one last great adventure, poor soul," Miz Opal agreed.

They discussed the lack of wind and rain and snow. Pleasant weather on all accounts, but "bad for business!" according to Dearest.

"And how are you getting on at Roselands?" Miz Opal asked, stirring two lumps of sugar into her tea.

"I miss my family," Millie said truthfully. "And . . . Christmas is coming, but it doesn't feel like Christmas at all. The house is decorated beautifully, and we have parties at least twice a week, and company almost every night . . . "

"And?" Miz Opal stopped stirring.

"And . . . it doesn't feel like Christmas," sighed Millie.

"I have heard that the Dinsmores are not a pious couple," Dearest said. "Though we've never had business with them, so I really can't say."

"Now, now," Miz Opal said. "If Jesus could bring Christmas to earth in a stable, then He can bring it to Roselands. Just invite Him to your celebrations there."

At those words, Millie's countenance brightened. "Thank you so much!" Millie said. "You have been more help than you can possibly know."

As Millie rode home in the buggy with Uncle Horace, she thought about the conversation. Miz Opal had put her finger right on the problem—and the solution! In the Keith home, Jesus was the center of their Christmas celebrations; at Roselands, they simply held an endless string of parties. *But I can bring Jesus to Roselands this Christmas!* Millie said to herself with a twinkle in her eye.

"What do you know about Christmas?" Millie asked Laylie the next morning, while the Dinsmore children were still in the schoolroom.

"We get a day off work," Laylie explained. "And material to make our clothes for the next year."

"Do you know why we celebrate Christmas?"

Laylie shook her head.

"It's because of Jesus," Millie explained. "We celebrate because God loved us so much that He sent His Son to die for us."

"Rachel read that to us from her Bible. Why would God do that? Send his boy to die?"

"Why did you give biscuits to your Merry Men?" Millie asked.

"Because they needed them," Laylie said. "I wanted to take care of them. And nobody else would give them any."

"Well, that's why God sent His Son!" Millie said. "Because we needed a Savior—someone to pay the price for our sins—and no one else could send one. It was wrong of you to steal, Laylie. But when you took care of your friends, you were being a little bit like Jesus."

"I liked it," Laylie said.

"That's because it's the way God created you to be. Would you like to give your friends gifts for Christmas?"

"Yes," Laylie said. "But I don't have anything to give."

"We will see about that," Millie said. She still had two pair of cotton bloomers and one petticoat that Claudina had given her. She pulled them out and laid them on the bed. "We can make rag dolls," Millie said. "Would your friends like that?"

"Maybe," Laylie said. "The girls anyway. But . . ."

"But?" said Millie.

"You're going to make them out of that?"

"Why not?" Millie said. "There is plenty of fabric for five large dolls."

"It's the wrong color," Laylie said.

"Oh!" Millie looked at the yards of white material. "I see what you mean. Perhaps Aunt Isabel will allow me to use scraps that her seamstresses have not thrown away." Aunt Isabel had no objection to Millie using the scraps from the sewing room, and soon Millie and Laylie were sorting through a wealth of remnants. There was enough fabric, buttons, and lace for a hundred fine dolls, but sturdy brown fabric for their faces and bodies was harder to find. Millie was hard-pressed to come up with cloth for four small dolls.

"That's enough," Laylie said. "The boys don't want dolls anyway."

Millie drew out patterns for the head and body and arms and legs on butcher's paper begged from Mrs. Brown. Laylie watched intently as Millie cut the fabric. She helped Millie stitch the seams along the sides of the arms and legs and Millie finished the body.

"Wait!" Laylie said when Millie started to stuff the doll's head with bits of rag. "I know something better to use." She led Millie to the warehouse where the cotton was weighed. The crop had already gone to market but there was still cotton to be had, puffy white handfuls still full of seeds. They gathered a bag full of the fluffy cotton and took it back to Millie's room. The cotton stuffing worked much better than rags. The doll's body was soft and huggable, and not as heavy as it would have been if it had been stuffed with scraps of cloth.

It took two days to finish the first small doll, working only in the mornings while Millie's cousins were in the schoolroom. Laylie spent the afternoons, no matter how drizzly or cold, in the woods with her friends. They built themselves a small shelter, well-hidden in the trees where they could have their own fire and cook corn cakes on a rock. Millie let Laylie do much of the work on the doll, showing her how to make curls of yarn for hair and sew on bright buttons for eyes. Then they used bits and pieces of satin and lace to make a fine gown. Last of all, Millie stitched on a sweet red smile.

"She's so pretty!" Laylie exclaimed when they finished the little doll. Millie had to agree. She was certainly not fine enough for a Dinsmore, but Fan would love a doll like this.

Once Laylie knew how it was done, she applied herself with diligence, working on the dolls every evening while Millie was entertaining at Isabel's parties. Millie enjoyed the company and laughter, but most of all she looked forward to talking with Charles each evening. He had a keen mind and was very well-educated and well-read. They were much in agreement about music, theater, and literature. Only when the subject turned to religion was it clear that there was no agreement between them. Millie had been careful not to mention Charles in her diary, not wanting to fuel Aunt Isabel's delusions of a match. But she mentioned him often in her prayers.

One day when the weather was unseasonably mild, Millie put together a sewing basket so that Laylie could work on wardrobes for the dolls in the garden. She took her sketchbook and they settled onto a bench under a spreading tree. Millie found herself thinking about Charles as she drew—wondering what he would say about a book she was reading—while Laylie grumbled over not having gifts for the boys.

"Hello, ladies."

Millie jumped. "Charles! We weren't expecting company!" She turned her sketchbook over quickly to hide the pointless doodles that covered the page.

"That is a fantastic doll," Charles said to Laylie. "May I see her?" He examined the doll in detail before handing her back. "I should think someone who could make a doll like that would be very proud."

"That's the problem," Millie explained. "Laylie can make dolls for girls, but what can she make for boys?"

"How many boys?" he inquired thoughtfully.

"Three," Laylie said, ticking them off on her fingers, "Will Scarlet, Alan-a-dale, and Friar Tuck."

"What? No Little John?" he teased.

"Little John is a girl," Millie explained. "Charles Landreth, meet Robin Hood."

"Charmed," Charles said, lifting his hat. "You have a problem with your band of merry rascals?"

"As their leader," Laylie said, "I wish to provide Christmas gifts," she sounded just as lofty as any nobleman, "but Millie said no more stealing."

"No *more* stealing?" asked Charles with surprise.

"I know," Laylie lowered her voice, as if that would separate them from Millie's meddling influence. "I don't see how I can be Robin Hood without stealing either. But Millie says that Christmas is about Jesus, and Jesus would not approve."

"I expect there are lots of people who would not approve," Charles said. "But perhaps we can think of something." He sat down beside Laylie. "I've got it! Every boy wants to be taller. Come with me." Millie and Laylie quickly packed the sewing basket, and Charles led the way around the house and up the kitchen steps.

"Hello, Phoebe," he said politely as he stepped in.

"Land o' Goshen! It's Charles Landreth!" Phoebe said. "I was sure I'd seen the last of you in this kitchen when Master Horace Jr. went away to school. You shore was the troublemaker! Keep your fingers out of my frosting now!"

"I wasn't a troublemaker," Charles said, scooping up a fingerful of sugar icing. "I was just full of ideas."

Laylie tried for a finger of icing, but Phoebe cracked her knuckles with the wooden spoon. Laylie jerked her hand back and stepped behind Charles. He picked up a spoon and attacked the icing again.

"I'm here about one of those good ideas now," he said, waving the spoon in the air. Still holding the spoon, he clasped his hands behind him, as if he were thinking. The spoon reappeared, licked clean. Millie frowned at him, but he only smiled, and dipped another spoonful. Millie took it from him and set it on the table. One spoonful of icing was quite enough for any little girl. Laylie peeked around him. She still had icing smudges on her face.

"Lucky you never got those older boys killed with your good ideas! Jumping off the roof of the barn with wings made of sticks!" said Phoebe, shaking her head.

"Horace landed in a haystack," he explained to Millie. "Man will fly someday, Phoebe," he said. "Take my word for it."

"And I s'pose they gonna make cannons that shoots out all o' my eggs, too?" She folded her arms and glared at him.

"No, I think that experiment saved mankind from similar mistakes forever," he said. "You have provided ample proof that eggs are better served in cakes and quiches."

"Then what are you doin' in my kitchen?" Phoebe asked.

"Looking for tin cans," Charles said. "I know Mrs. Dinsmore is fond of serving canned vegetables when they are out of season. I believe we had some last night."

"Maybe a few in the rubbish," Phoebe grumbled. "If you weren't a favorite of Miss Isabel, I'd throw you right out of here!"

"No doubt!" Charles said, sorting though the trash. He pulled out two empty tin cans of the same size. "These will do," he said. "Don't throw any more cans away. Miss Millie wants them all washed and then saved."

"I do?" Millie asked in surprise.

"Of course you do," Charles said with a smile. "You just don't know it yet. Come on."

The next stop was the smithy behind the stables. Charles borrowed a hammer and nail and pierced the sides of each can twice. He made loops of twine and fed them through the holes and then tied knots so that they would not slip back through.

"Watch this," he said to Laylie. He set his foot on top of one of the cans and stood up, balancing on the can. He set his other foot on the other can, and then holding the loops in his hands, started to walk.

"Stilts!" Millie said.

"Can-ilts," he corrected. "There were some advantages to growing up with an aunt who refuses to spend money on frivolities such as toys!"

When Laylie stood on the cans, she was almost as tall as Millie. She clumped around the stable yard, delighted with her height. Charles laughed as she bumped her head on a low tree branch and then toddled out into the yard. Millie realized suddenly that he was treating Laylie just as he would any child—not as a servant, or someone less than himself.

"Charles," Millie said, searching his face. "You do know Laylie is a slave?"

"A slave?" He winked. "No! I thought she was Robin Hood!"

"I like him," Laylie said when Charles was gone. "He reminds me of Luke."

I like him too, Millie admitted to herself. *Maybe a little too much. Was it only two months ago that Pappa warned me about losing my heart to a young man?*

"Come on, Laylie, let's put the can-ilts away before someone sees them."

They returned to the house and hid the cans under Millie's bed in a box with the dolls Laylie was making.

That night, Laylie set to work on yet another doll dress while Millie opened her diary. *Yes, here it is,* she said. "*Jesus, please hold my heart in Your hand. Don't let me give it or any piece of it away. I want YOU to give it away in Your time, to the right person. Please hold it tight, lock it up, and keep the key. October 8, 1836.*" Millie sighed. *I will be sixteen in a week. Sixteen is too young for romance, isn't it?* she asked herself. She was sure that Mamma would say it was. And Pappa would ask if the young man knew Jesus as his King. But Aunt Isabel would point out that many young women her age were engaged; some were even married.

The memory of Charles's smile crept into her mind, and Millie quickly snapped her diary shut. *Lord, I gave You my heart,* she prayed silently. *Don't let me take it back and give it to another!*

CHAPTER

7

The First Cut

*Let us continually offer to God a
sacrifice of praise — the fruit of
lips that confess his name. And
do not forget to do good and to
share with others, for with
such sacrifices God
is pleased.*

HEBREWS 13:15–16

The First Cut

With gifts for Laylie's Merry Midgets well taken care of, Millie turned her thoughts to what she could give the young girl. She was willing to spend Uncle Horace's money on gifts for the Dinsmore children, but for Laylie she wanted something special, something of her own that didn't belong to Roselands. The problem was, Millie had very little in the way of worldly possessions — the clothes she had brought with her, her art supplies, and a few books. These last she examined carefully, thinking that a book of her own would be a wonderful gift for Laylie. But the *History of the World* and *Studies in the Plant and Animal Kingdom*, while fascinating, hardly seemed to be the kind of reading she would enjoy.

Laylie was still working her way through *Robin Hood*, or rather was working her way through it yet again. Millie had offered to borrow another book from Uncle Horace's library for her, and even suggested a few titles, but Laylie had refused. *Robin Hood* was the book she wanted. Millie picked it up off the desk where Laylie always placed it when she was done reading. Robin was quite a handsome fellow she decided, in his green cloak and woodsman's cap. *A green cloak! That's it!*

Millie went to her chiffonier and pushed the new dresses aside until she found the emerald green silk she had brought from Pleasant Plains. She held the cover of the book against the dress. It was the exact color of Robin's cape! She felt the heavy silk and sighed. This dress had been a gift twice, once from Millie to Rhoda Jane, and once from Rhoda Jane to Millie. Rhoda Jane had worn this dress to her first-ever Christmas social and had said, "It was the first time I knew that Jesus loved me." *But this could be the very thing that shows Laylie that Jesus loves her!* Still, Millie agonized over the decision. *I promised Rhoda Jane that I would wear this dress for a special occasion. Would Rhoda Jane approve of me making it into a cloak for Robin Hood?* Millie laughed at the thought. Rhoda Jane was the most practical girl she had ever met. She had no sense of romance whatsoever. She could almost hear her saying, "Get the scissors! I'll help!"

Millie took her scissors from the sewing basket and bit her lip. One cut. One cut and she would be committed. She set the scissors down. *I promised I would wear it.* She pulled her dress off and slipped the green gown over her head. When it was fastened up, it was a perfect fit, even though she had made it for her thirteenth birthday. *I look better in it now than I would have then,* she decided. She had grown an inch and a half at least, and didn't need heels to keep the hem from dragging on the floor.

Millie twirled in front of the mirror. She curtsied to an imaginary partner, and began to dance. *I wonder what Charles would think of this dress? It does make me look older.*

Suddenly tears came to Millie's eyes, and she knelt in the middle of the floor.

Jesus, Charles Landreth is creeping into my heart. I can't tell Mamma or even write it in my diary because Aunt Isabel would read it, and I can't bear for her to know. I want You to know that I believe Your promises. That You have the best life planned for me, and I must not turn away from You. Help me be faithful no matter what. Jesus, let my heart always belong to You!

Millie went to her desk and opened her Bible, searching for comfort and guidance. She flipped from book to book, looking for a verse that would help. Mamma would know just where to look, or Pappa or Aunt Wealthy, but she couldn't think of one verse that would help. *If only I could talk to Mamma about what is happening in my heart!* Wiping away her tears, she tried reading again, and there it was in Psalm 139—the perfect verse, right under her thumb. "Search me, O God, and know my heart; test me and know my anxious thoughts. See if there is any offensive way in me, and lead me in the way everlasting."

Millie wrote the verse out on a page of her diary. She took the green dress off and slipped back into her everyday clothes. She picked up her scissors and made the first cut quickly, not stopping until she had separated the skirt from the blouse. Then she made the fabric into a bundle to carry to the sewing room, where she could work without Laylie seeing her. She was halfway down the hall when she turned around and ran back. Her diary was still open to the verse she had just written, the ink hardly dry on the page. She tore the page out, folded it, and put it in her pocket. She had memorized the short verse by the time she reached the sewing room, but every time she put her hand in her pocket, she remembered to ask God to examine and guard her heart.

Millie received two letters from home on her sixteenth birthday, and it was the best present she could have asked for. Although Millie mailed letters faithfully every week, winter had settled in over the northern states, slowing and often stopping the stagecoaches that carried the mail.

Millie put her mother's letter aside, to be read last, and unfolded the one from Rhoda Jane. Gordon said the coats on the squirrels were heavy, and that predicted a cold winter. He also said that plans were being made for a delightful winter social — and sleigh rides, of course; the ponds and streams were already sheathed in ice. Millie continued reading, smiling to herself at her friend's words:

You know from my last letter, dear friend, that Nicholas Ransquate had purchased yet another new hat — a sure sign that he was about to propose. He was driving the gossips mad by wandering the byways in said hat, a volume of poetry in his hand and a dreamy look on his face. Some say that he has lost his courage at last, and is afraid to approach the young lady. Others point out that he has proposed to every available girl in town.

Your own mother, Millie, smiles and says that Nicholas has fallen in love at last, and it has made him shy. Nicholas shy! Can you imagine! I pray for him daily. What a terrible thing it would be to fall in love at last, and after so many practice proposals, not to be able to utter the words.

Whatever the case, Nicholas's hat came to naught. He was wearing it last Wednesday and reading his poetry when he wandered across the ice of the pond behind the Union Hotel. The ice was not thick, and by the time he realized where he was, it was too late. He made a mad dash for safety, but the ice gave way, and he plunged into the freezing water. He could not pull himself out as the ice kept breaking.

Fortunately, Damaris happened to be in the neighborhood and heard his desperate shout as he fell in. She dashed to Mrs. Prior's wash, which was in a basket on her back porch, and grabbed a pair of bloomers. Edging as near as she dared to the hole in the ice, she threw one leg of the bloomers to Nicholas and hauled him out, saving him from death — if not humiliation.

The First Cut

It's a good thing it was Mrs. Prior's bloomers she lit upon. The good woman believes in sturdy cotton, and her seams are legendary for their durability. A garment may grow thin and wear away, but Mrs. Prior's needlework will remain!

Nicholas's marvelous new hat was left bobbing on the water, and has since frozen firmly into the ice. His poetry is lost to the depths. And Nicholas himself is confined to bed, battling a severe cold.

Millie stopped reading long enough to pray for Nicholas, even though she knew that the crisis must be long past, since the letter had been so long in arriving. Her mother's letter was warm and comforting, expressing delight that Millie was enjoying her stay at Roselands, assuring her that her parents prayed for her daily and that her sisters longed for her return—especially Zillah, who read with excitement the descriptions Millie sent of her new wardrobe. There was a note in Zillah's handwriting at the bottom of the page.

Dearest, dearest sister. May I borrow your rose gown when you return? It sounds so lovely when you describe it. You will be back in April, just in time for Easter. I think I have a bonnet that would match!

Back home for Easter! Millie thought, staring out the window with longing. *It seems an eternity away.*

On Christmas Eve, the Dinsmore parlor was filled with neighbors, some merry and some not. It seemed the entire town had been invited. Mrs. Landreth wandered from group to group speculating on the cost of the decorations and delicacies and making comments about starving children in China. Mrs. Travilla sat quietly in the corner, attended by Old Rachel. The kitchen slaves and waiters wore harried, worried expressions, glancing at Isabel if the slightest thing went wrong.

The Dinsmore children were allowed at the party for a change, and Millie was surprised at how well they behaved. Adelaide was quite grown up, joining in conversations with her elders. Louise and Lora were content to be admired in their new Christmas dresses. Walter and Enna were charming and sweet, and Arthur stayed very quiet, sneaking time and again to the dessert tray.

Millie had been planning her own part in the evening ever since the day she had spoken to Miz Opal. Time and again she started to put her plan into action, and time and again she hesitated. She almost lost her chance when Arthur complained of a stomachache and Isabel directed that all of the children be sent to bed. "May they stay up just a little longer?" Millie asked. "I would like to show them how their cousins in Pleasant Plains celebrate Christmas Eve."

Isabel looked as if she was going to say no, but Uncle Horace intervened. "Surely they can stay up a little longer," he said. "In the spirit of the season."

Millie pulled her Bible out of the piano bench, where she had placed it earlier in the day. "I need a narrator," she said. "Could you be persuaded to read, Mr. Lochneer?" She offered him the Bible.

"Oh!" Otis said. "I would be delighted . . . but my voice!" Otis hesitated. "My throat is all scratches and squeaks. Let me see . . . ." He struck a pose and said, "Me me me me!" in his deepest voice. He thumped his chest and tried again. "Me me mee-eek!" his voice broke. "Oh dear! I can't Millie, I just can't!"

Charles shook his head and took the Bible from Otis's hand. "I have been known to read in public," he said.

Several of the young ladies clapped. *Lord,* Millie prayed. *Help me get through this!* She pulled Charles to the side. "You are not supposed to write in books," he whispered, as she showed him the faint line she had drawn under the passages he was to read. "Though this one seems ready to fall out of its binding."

"Just be careful with it," Millie said. "I am going to be playing the piano. When I nod, you start reading. I'll nod again when you are to stop."

"How am I supposed to see you nod if I am reading?" he asked.

Millie's ears grew warm. *I didn't think about that.*

"How about this?" he offered. "I'll sit on the bench beside you and face the crowd. When you want me to stop reading, elbow me."

"All right," Millie said, after a moment's hesitation. She called the children to come closer and sit on the floor, then seated herself at the piano and started to play softly.

She nodded at Charles, and he began to read from the second chapter of Luke, " 'In those days Caesar Augustus issued a decree that a census should be taken of the entire Roman world. And everyone went to his own town to register. So Joseph also went up from the town of Nazareth in Galilee to Judea, to Bethlehem the town of David, because he belonged to the house and line of David. He went there to register with Mary, who was pledged to be married to him and was expecting a child. While they were there, the time came for the baby to be born, and she gave birth to her firstborn, a son. She wrapped him in cloths and placed him in a manger, because there was no room for them in the inn.' Ouuuf!"

"Sorry," Millie whispered as she struck the first chord of "Silent Night." Mrs. Travilla's voice was the first one raised, and soon the whole room was singing the hymn, and then Charles read again, through the visit of the angels to the shepherds. Millie didn't look around, but many voices joined in singing "Angels We Have Heard on High."

They continued on until the story of the Savior's birth was told in narration and song. Charles's reading was brilliant, full of depth and emotion. When at last they finished, the room was very still, and even the children were hushed. Millie turned around to face her audience for the first time. The entire room was full. Even the kitchen servants had come in to hear the story.

"And that is how we celebrate the Savior's birth in Pleasant Plains," Millie said with a sweet smile. The room burst into applause.

"Let's see your frontiersman beat that," Charles said, taking a bow.

"Which frontiersman?" asked Millie.

"I was speaking of your fiancé. Do you have more than one?"

"Fiancé?" Isabel had come up to share in the applause as if the whole performance had been her idea. "Don't be absurd, Charles. Millie has no fiancé. She is totally available!"

Millie wished that she could sink into the floor and disappear, but she just kept smiling.

"I must be going," Charles said at last. "It's been delightful, Isabel, but I have things to attend to early."

The children were kissed and sent to bed, and the crowd began to break up. Coats and cloaks were collected, and drivers hurried from the kitchen to their coaches.

Millie stood with the Dinsmores on the porch, bidding each guest goodbye.

"Beautifully done, dear," Mrs. Travilla said. "Your parents would be proud."

After the last guest had said goodbye, Millie noticed someone standing alone in the dark. She took a few steps out of the light before she recognized the form. "I thought you had gone, Mr. Landreth." Charles was gazing up at a sky that blazed with stars.

"They are beautiful," he said.

"Isn't it amazing to think that they are the same stars that shone over the manger?" Millie asked.

"How can you believe that story is true?" Charles asked. "There are so many legends and fairy tales."

"No fairy, no creature of legend or myth has ever changed the world. Can you deny that Jesus has?"

"He was a great man, and a good teacher," said Charles.

"He was *God*," Millie said. "He created the stars. And He gave you the eyes with which to see them, and the heart that yearns for their beauty."

"Goodnight, Millie," Charles said. He settled his hat on his head and started toward the stables to find his horse.

Laylie was speechless when she saw the box wrapped in bright paper and tied with a bow at the foot of her bed the next morning.

"It's for you," Millie said. "Open it!"

Millie's Faithful Heart

All of the agony over the decision to make that first cut with the scissors was erased by the look on Laylie's face as she held up her cloak. Millie helped her fasten it around her neck, and then put the feathered cap on her head. Laylie examined herself in the mirror, and very slowly a smile spread across her face. "Can I wear it when I take my gifts to the woods?"

"Of course!" Millie said.

The rest of the morning was filled with extravagant gifts for the Dinsmore children from their parents—toys and trinkets, a pony for Arthur. Isabel received jewelry from Uncle Horace, a glittering necklace and matching earrings. Millie had books and new art supplies, but nothing she received could compare with the gift of the smile on Laylie's face.

"Millie," Laylie said that night after prayers, "did you mean it when you said you were taking me home with you?"

"Of course I did," Millie said.

"I'm glad your cough's better, then," Laylie said. "I wish we could leave now."

"I do, too," Millie replied. "But we have to wait for Uncle Horace to escort us. Ladies do not simply up and wander across the country on their own."

"Are you sure we are going?"

"Yes, I am," Millie said. "Why wouldn't we?"

"Because you might decide to stay and marry Mr. Landreth," Laylie said. "I heard the girls in the kitchen talking about it."

"That is nonsense," Millie said, slipping her hand in her pocket to grip the folded paper.

CHAPTER

8

A Big Lie

"The serpent deceived me, and I ate."

GENESIS 3:13

A Big Lie

January of 1837 was unusually mild, having few days too cold or wet for Millie to take her exercise outside with Laylie in the mornings. The climate and exercise worked wonders for her health. Although she was often tired from Aunt Isabel's endless parties—some of which she spent with her hand in her pocket the entire time—her cough had disappeared. By the end of January, Millie was not rubbing the verse in her pocket quite so much. It seemed clear that Charles was not foolish enough to fall in love with a sixteen-year-old. He missed several of Isabel's parties in a row, and Millie was so glad—or so she told herself—that she cried herself to sleep on each occasion.

She talked more and more to Laylie, treating the child like one of her own little sisters. The two, one in a green cloak and the other in the most stylish of dresses and hats and carrying a parasol, traipsed the pathways of Roselands while the Dinsmore children were at their studies. Laylie had given up *Robin Hood*, if not her costume or her Merry Men, in favor of the *Leatherstocking Tales*, which Millie borrowed for her.

Laylie talked endlessly about the frontier, and spoke of Don, Cyril, and Fan as if she had known them all of her life. When Millie received a letter from home, Laylie sat at her feet and laughed or cried with her as Millie read it aloud. Rhoda Jane's letters always brought peals of laughter.

My dear friend, I'm sure there is no location on earth as romantic as our own Pleasant Plains. There will be a wedding in the spring, and this is how it came about:

Millie's Faithful Heart

Nicholas's cold deepened into pneumonia. The Reverend and Mrs. Lord had brought the poor bachelor to their own home, the better to care for him, and laid him on a cot in the parlor. Reverend and Mrs. Lord as well as Damaris attended what we all felt were to be his last hours on earth.

Delirious with fever, he tossed on his bed, calling out for his hat. All at once he sat up straight, ghostlike in his white nightshirt. "Cannot . . . cannot ask . . . ." he said, and fell back as if he were drifting away.

Damaris rushed out of the house, seized the ax from the woodpile, and hacked the hat, encased as it was in a block of ice, out of the pond. She lifted it, ice and all, in her arms, and staggered to the house, pushed the door open, and fell on her knees beside his cot. "Don't you dare die, Mr. Ransquate. I won't have it!" she cried. "I've brought the hat, and I am not leaving without a proposal!"

Nicholas was revived, and though he did not have enough breath for the full one hour proposal he had planned, he did manage to squeak out, "Marry me?" And Damaris fell into his arms. His health took an immediate turn for the better. Have you ever heard anything so romantic in your life?

Millie worked diligently at making dresses for Laylie, as she would need several for the trip. She had worked at Mamma's side for many years making clothing for the younger children, but it had never been her full responsibility before. She finished the pink dress that she had put off until after Christmas, as well as a blue dress and an apron. Laylie had become quite good with her needle, as good as Adah at least, and delighted in helping make her own clothes.

A Big Lie

Though Millie tried not to count the days, she was filled with inexpressible joy in late February when, on one of their long walks, they came unexpectedly upon a pink dogwood in full and glorious bloom. The waxy blossoms looked like little bits of heaven tangled in the branches of a tree.

"Do you see this, Laylie?" Millie said, breaking off a twig and tucking it in Laylie's hair. "It means it's almost time to go home! Pleasant Plains is still covered with snow and ice, but even there the buds are beginning to swell!"

"Where will I live when we get there?" Laylie asked.

"With me, of course," Millie said. She had not written home about the girl. She was sure Aunt Isabel read her letters before they were posted, and there was so much to say about Laylie that she did not know where to start, or where to stop. Mamma and Pappa would certainly be surprised when she showed up with a new sister, but she was sure they would welcome the child into their home.

"When are we going to leave?" asked Laylie.

"In less than a month," Millie assured her. "And it will take us a month to get home."

"I don't know what my Merry Men will do without me," Laylie said. "Maybe I will have to come back for them one day."

"Maybe," Millie said uncertainly, "but not one day soon."

Uncle Horace ordered his affairs and prepared for the journey, and suggested that they take Adelaide along for the trip. Adelaide was elated and Isabel indifferent, not having the least desire to make the journey herself. Millie was delighted, as Adelaide had quickly become her favorite cousin—and the only one she would really miss. Not only that, but Adelaide's visit made it possible to prepare things in Pleasant Plains for Laylie's arrival. She wrote to her mother and sisters asking that they take special care in preparing the guest room for a young girl's visit.

Millie was sketching on the lawn one afternoon when Charles Landreth came down the path, whistling and swinging his cane. Her heart gave a small lurch, but she pinched herself. Charles had not spent much time at Roselands in the last weeks, and she had forgotten to put her Scripture verse in her pocket.

"There are Carolina parakeets nesting in a tree at the bottom of the garden," he said. "Have you seen them?"

"No," Millie said, gathering up her art supplies. "I would love to." She looked around for Laylie. "Laylie! Let's go down to the end of the garden," Millie called. "Did you have business with Uncle Horace?" she asked Charles.

"Of a sort," Charles said. "And it went very well."

"What did?" asked Millie.

"The business. Look! Did you see that flash of green?"

"Laylie! Do not throw rocks at birds!" yelled Millie.

"Laylie, would you run back to the house and bring my coat?" Charles said. "I seem to have forgotten it."

Laylie was off in a flash. Millie suddenly realized that she was alone with Charles.

"I understand you will be leaving us soon, Miss Keith," he said.

"Yes. I am going home in three weeks."

"Then I have something to say to you. I would have asked your father, but he is not available so I consulted with your uncle and received his approval."

Millie's heart leapt, and then froze. *Surely Charles is not about to propose to me?*

"I saw one!" Millie said, turning away.

"One what?" Charles looked over his shoulder.

"A Carolina parakeet!" Millie started to walk away.

"Millie!" he caught her hand. "Hear me out. You know what I am going to say, don't you? I am in love with you. You are the only one for me, I am sure of it. And you are in love with me, too."

"I'm what?" she cried.

"In love with me," he said with certainty.

"I am . . . " Millie was sure she was going to say, "I am not!" But somehow only the first two words came out.

"So when will you marry me?" Charles asked, smiling with a twinkle in his eyes.

Millie's eyes filled with tears. "I'm not going to marry you . . . my . . . my parents wouldn't approve." *My parents? Why did I say that? That's not the reason I can't marry him at all.* Millie's head was spinning. *What is the reason?* She had been so busy pretending that she didn't love Charles that she had not even thought about marriage at all. She hadn't let herself think about it.

"I know you are young," Charles said, "but I am willing to wait."

"No!" Millie said. There was a sob bubbling up in her, and she couldn't help it.

"When you are in love with a man you are not supposed to say *no*," Charles explained. "You are supposed to say *yes*."

Millie turned and ran.

"Millie! I didn't mean . . . " but Millie didn't hear his words through her sobs.

She wiped the tears from her cheeks before she entered the house, but they were still blurring her eyes. Aunt Isabel was sitting in the parlor looking just as Fan's kitten had the day it swallowed Millie's pet sparrow. Uncle Horace was standing behind her with a smile on his face. The smile faded as he took in the sight of Millie's tears.

"My dear girl . . . "

"You haven't turned him down!" Isabel said, standing up. "The catch of the season! Every young lady in the county is trying to win his heart! You are not going to get another chance at a match like that, Millie Keith!"

Millie opened her mouth, but no words would come out. *Never another chance with Charles!* She simply shook her head and ran up the stairs to her room. She tried to read her Bible, but her tears seemed to wash the words from the page.

The shadows of afternoon had turned twilight blue when Laylie came into the room at last. She crept up on the bed and put her arms around Millie.

"Something's wrong with this old world," she said. "Just wrong. And there's nobody can fix it."

Millie knew she should say "Jesus can." Yet nothing but sobs came out when she opened her mouth.

"Now, now," Laylie said, stroking her head. Millie fell asleep in her arms.

Uncle Horace, looking awkward and uncomfortable, brought Millie a breakfast tray the next morning.

"I would not have given Charles permission to speak to you if I had known how you felt. Isabel was sure that you loved him."

"My father would never approve of my marrying a man who was not a Christian, Uncle Horace," said Millie.

"But do you love him?" Millie didn't answer. "I don't understand it," said Uncle Horace, shaking his head. "Charles is a fine man, Millie. He loves you and has ample means to support you. I fear that your over-devotion to these religious ideas will end in as much joy as Mrs. Landreth's."

"Perhaps I will be like Aunt Wealthy," Millie said. "She seems happy in her choices."

Uncle Horace simply shook his head. "I apologize for allowing a situation that was painful for you, Millie. Perhaps with time, you will reconsider. You need to think about this carefully. Think what it could mean to your family. Isabel does not know their circumstances, but I do. Charles Landreth is a very wealthy young man. If you marry him, your father need no longer worry about his legal practice making a profit. Your mother can have servants, and your brothers will go to the finest schools. Your sisters will have opportunities for marriage that they never would have had before. I know you are young and idealistic. But please, as your father is not here, take the advice of someone to whom your parents entrusted you. Accept Charles Landreth's proposal."

"I have already turned it down," Millie said.

"You still have some weeks here, and Charles was adamant about his love," Uncle Horace said. "If I were to write a letter . . . "

"No," Millie said. "I can't, Uncle."

The color had gone out of spring for Millie, replaced with the gray of ashes and the taste of dust. She had found the Scriptures she knew her Mamma and Pappa would lead her to—Scriptures about not being joined together with someone who did not belong to the Lord.

Millie's Faithful Heart

But why? Charles Landreth was the finest young man she had ever met. Surely, if she married him, it would not be long before he became a Christian? He would see her faith, and go with her to church. But God's Word said no. *Jesus,* Millie prayed, *help me stay faithful to You, no matter what I feel. No matter what I want.* Her only solace was the fact that her time at Roselands was limited, and every sunset brought her closer to the time she would return to Pleasant Plains.

"Well, Charles has left for Charleston, I hear," Isabel said one morning when she found Millie in the sewing room. "Otis has dragged him there to find parties and young ladies to distract him, I'm sure." Isabel had not entertained since the proposal, and after her announcement of Charles's departure, she avoided meeting Millie in the halls. She was never present at breakfast. Millie waited for her to reappear, but as the time for her departure drew near, she decided that she had to seek her aunt out. She found Isabel lounging on her bed in her dressing gown.

"May I come in, Aunt Isabel?"

Isabel nodded and Millie entered the room. "I don't suppose you have come to apologize?" Isabel said. "After everything I have done for you, to simply turn down Charles! I can't imagine your mother would be pleased with the way you have abused my hospitality."

"I apologize if I have offended you, Aunt Isabel," Millie said. "I have appreciated your hospitality more than you can know."

"Really?" Isabel sat up. "Then stay until Charles comes back. Let him give you one more chance. I'm sure he will!"

"I cannot," Millie said. *Please, Lord, let me be gone before he comes back!* "I will be leaving myself in a week," Millie said.

"I have begun packing. I was wondering if you could provide the papers for Laylie?"

"Papers?" Isabel's eyes narrowed.

"You said that you would provide her papers before I left."

"Why would I do that?" asked Isabel.

"Because . . ." Millie felt a tickle of fear inside. "Because you promised her to me if I would play at your parties. I have done so, and they have been brilliant. You said so yourself."

"You must have mistaken my intent," Isabel said. "I never meant to *give* the child to you. Just to let you have her as your servant while you were here."

"That is not true!" Millie said. "We had an agreement."

"An agreement of that kind would need to have witnesses, I believe," Isabel said. "Have you any?"

"I will speak to Uncle Horace about it."

"Horace will believe me," Isabel said, smiling. "He always does. After you leave, I will return the child to Meadshead. I will have no use for her here."

CHAPTER 9

A Change in Plans

In his heart a man plans his course, but the Lord determines his steps.

PROVERBS 16:9

*M*illie walked across the garden, trying to make sense of the thoughts and emotions that raged within her. Surely Uncle Horace would never allow the child to be sent back to Meadshead — not after what had happened to Luke?

But it would be only slightly better for Laylie to stay at Roselands. If she got sent to the fields, she would work twelve or fourteen hours every day. If she were allowed to stay in the house, she would be under Isabel's eyes and subject to Arthur's tantrums. Either way, she would never have books, never have an education, never be able to pursue the dreams God put in her heart.

In her heart. Millie stopped. *Is God punishing me? I promised Him my heart, and then I let Charles Landreth seep in.*

She thought back over the last few months, every laugh, smile, and party. Every decision she had made that led to this point. If Charles had not proposed, Laylie would be on her way to Pleasant Plains within the week. *Did I encourage Charles? Did I flirt? Laylie was depending on me, and I failed. Maybe God is punishing me.* Millie pushed the thoughts from her mind. *Of course He's not. God doesn't punish His children — He disciplines us because we need correction. Surely He will send a miracle now and let Laylie go to Pleasant Plains with me.*

Millie sank to her knees on the new spring grass. "Lord, please change Aunt Isabel's heart," she prayed earnestly. "I can't leave Laylie here. I just can't."

That night, Laylie chattered herself to sleep, talking about the trip and Fan, and worrying about Bobforshort, the hound pup Uncle Horace had sent to Cyril and Don. Laylie didn't like dogs, especially hound dogs — the kind who tracked people through the swamps. Millie tried to find the words to explain to Laylie that she wasn't going to Pleasant Plains after all, but she couldn't.

When Laylie was finally asleep, Millie wrapped her shawl around her shoulders, crept down the stairs, and walked into the night. The moon was a celestial orange over the horizon. As it rose, it became a silver disc so bright it washed the stars from the sky.

"Lord, show me Your plan," Millie prayed. "What am I supposed to do?" Millie sat in silence, wondering what God might have her do. *Tell her again about Jesus*, was the only thought that came to her. *Why, of course! It's the most important thing I could ever give her! And I have put it off, thinking that Mamma and Pappa would do it when I took her home.*

Millie still read the Bible aloud to Laylie every night, but she had mainly focused on stories her own brothers and sisters loved—Noah and the Ark, David and Goliath, Daniel and the Lion's Den. All of them taught important things about God, of course, but they didn't directly explain how to become a Christian or why you needed to be one. *Faith comes from hearing the message, and the message is heard through the word of Christ, says Romans 10:17. But which words? Surely if she didn't listen to Rachel, she will not listen to me.* Millie walked and prayed until the dewfall dampened her shawl before she went inside.

The next day Millie immersed herself in prayer and Bible reading with an urgency she had never felt before, searching for just the right Scriptures for Laylie. She was surprised at how many of the words she needed were verses her Mamma had given her to memorize, many from the book of Romans. "Therefore, just as sin entered the world through one man, and death through sin, and in this way death came to all men, because all sinned"; "For all have sinned and fall short of the glory of God"; and "For the wages of sin is death, but the gift of God is eternal life in Christ Jesus our Lord." *If Laylie doesn't understand what sin is, how can she understand why she needs a Savior?*

Millie prepared very carefully for her Bible reading that night. As Laylie brushed out Millie's hair, Millie read from Genesis the story of Adam and Eve. She explained that sin was breaking God's laws, and then read to Laylie Scripture verses from the book of Romans one by one.

"Is hating Mr. Borse a sin?" Laylie asked when Millie had finished.

"Yes," Millie said. "When you hate someone, it is like the sin of murder in your heart. You can't keep love for God and murder in your heart at the same time. But there is good news. Even though all of us have sinned, God loves us. Listen to this." She opened her Bible to John 3:16, even though she knew it by heart. She wanted to be sure Laylie knew that these were God's own words. "For God so loved the world that he gave his one and only Son, that whoever believes in him shall not perish but have eternal life."

"Mr. Borse is the worst sinner I know," Laylie said. "Does Jesus love him?"

"Yes," Millie said, her heart sinking. This conversation was not going as she had planned at all. "Jesus loves everyone, and wants them to turn from their sin and be saved. But He does not love the evil things Mr. Borse does."

Laylie shook her head. "I don't see how anybody could love *him*," she said. "Goodnight."

Millie's Faithful Heart

Time after time over the next week, Millie tried to open her mouth and talk about salvation with Laylie, but each time she faltered on the words. *Should I tell Laylie that she might not come to Pleasant Plains first? Then surely she won't listen. If I speak of a Savior first, then won't Laylie feel betrayed when she is left behind?*

Three days before Millie was to leave, she was again strolling in the garden, absorbed in prayer, trying desperately not to worry. She had been expecting a miracle, a change of heart—*something* that would provide a way for Laylie to go with her. Aunt Isabel was not only unchanging, she was positively cold. Millie had just decided that she had to ask Uncle Horace for help again when she turned a corner and almost ran into him.

"I should like to have chat with you, Millie," he said. "If you have time."

"Of course, Uncle Horace," Millie said, as he matched his longer stride to hers.

"I have received terrible news," Uncle Horace said. "News that will affect you, I am afraid."

Millie's hand flew to her heart. "Not my family?"

"No, no! I am sorry to have worded it in such a way. Your family, as far as I know, is well and expecting your return. Therein lies the problem. I have received word from my solicitor, and I must delay the trip to Pleasant Plains." Millie was too stunned to speak, but Uncle Horace didn't seem to notice. "A letter arrived from Louisiana yesterday, bringing the news of a death."

"I'm sorry, Uncle Horace. Was it a close relation?"

He waved his hand in the air. "No relation at all. In fact, I did not know the gentleman. He was the guardian left to watch over Elsie and her property. Horace Jr. cannot come home to set the estate in order. In his absence, the responsibility falls upon me. I must not only look after the estate, but the child as well. It involves an immediate journey to New Orleans and then on to Viamede, the Grayson plantation, to get matters settled."

"Are you suggesting that I stay at Roselands until your return, or have you found another escort for me?" asked Millie.

"Neither. I must bring the child home with me. Leaving her at Viamede with servants is not possible, and, being a young child, she cannot be sent to boarding school yet. So until Horace Jr. returns, Roselands will have to be her home. I am suggesting that you go with me to retrieve her." He glanced at her hopefully.

New Orleans is over eight hundred miles away, almost as far as Pleasant Plains! Mamma and Pappa are expecting me. This will delay my arrival by months.

"Can't Aunt Isabel go with you?" Millie asked.

Uncle Horace sighed. "Isabel is justifiably upset. I will be bringing a child, who is hardly her social equal, to live with our own children. Who knows how this girl has been raised, or what sort of creature she is? As I have said before, Horace Jr. is in no way Isabel's son. As his father, I must live with his mistakes, but I will try to make it as painless as possible for Isabel. She will remain here."

"Do you mean that you did not ask her to accompany you?" Millie asked.

Uncle Horace gave her an exasperated glance. "She declined."

"Poor little motherless Elsie!" Millie's eyes began to fill with tears, but she wasn't sure whether they were for the mother the child had lost or the future that awaited the little girl at Roselands. "Will Cousin Horace be home soon?"

Millie's Faithful Heart

"I hardly think so," Uncle Horace said. "He has some years to study yet."

They walked on in silence for some time. "Will you accompany me to Louisiana? I have already sent a letter to your parents explaining the delay and promising your safe return at the soonest opportunity."

"I will," Millie said. "I'm sure my parents would want me to help you and little Elsie in any way possible. I have but one request: May I take Laylie with me?"

Uncle Horace pursed his lips. "I don't see why you should not," he said at last. "One does grow used to the habits and personality of a servant."

Their walk had taken them all the way around the garden path and back to the house. "Since you are already packed, I see no reason why we should not leave tomorrow. Could you send Adelaide to me? I know she was looking forward to our journey, but I do not feel she should accompany us this time."

Millie found Adelaide, Louise, and Lora in the entryway with Isabel, dressed and apparently on their way to town for a shopping excursion.

"Pardon me, Aunt Isabel," Millie said. "Uncle Horace has requested that Adelaide meet him in the garden."

Isabel picked up her dainty gloves as if she hadn't heard a word that Millie had spoken.

"Aunt Isabel?" Millie queried. "May Adelaide go to her father?"

"It's the issue of that *child*, isn't it?" She pulled one glove on, none too gently. "Horace promised that she would not interfere with my family, but see? She has already! Does he expect me to wait while he attends *her* business? I won't do it." She pulled on the other glove and checked her reflection in the mirror. "You may go to your father, Adelaide. I will see you on my return."

"Mother, please wait," Adelaide pleaded. "It will only take a moment, I am sure."

"What child, Mother?" Lora asked.

Isabel's porcelain skin flushed rose pink and her lips pressed together.

"Mother, what's wrong?" Adelaide asked in alarm.

"Your father is what's wrong. How can he expect me to accept that child into my home? It's not enough that I've been tormented with a stepson. Must I have a step . . . " She turned away from the mirror.

"Step what, Mother?" Louise asked.

"What child?" Lora stomped her feet.

"Horace Jr.'s child! You may as well know; there is no way to avoid it."

"Is he married?" Louise asked.

"I shouldn't wonder that you are surprised," Isabel said. "Your father tried to hide it even from me, but I have ways of finding out." Here she glanced at Millie, and the blush that had fled her face did not have the decency to return. "Horace was married, and to a very common girl. She died soon after giving birth to their child."

"An orphan baby!" Adelaide clapped her hands. "Can we care for it?"

"*It* is a little girl," Millie told her cousin. "She's just four years old and her name is Elsie Dinsmore."

"What a sweet name," Louise said.

"What relation is she to us, Millie?" asked Lora. "Is she a cousin like you?"

"No, silly," Millie said. "You are her aunts!"

125

Millie's Faithful Heart

"That means Mother's a . . . *grandmother!*" Lora said with a laugh.

Isabel gave Millie a withering look. "I certainly am not! I never want to hear you say that again, Lora. Elsie Dinsmore is not related to me in the least. Now go to your father, Adelaide. We shall show you our purchases when we return." Isabel swept out of the room, Louise and Lora in tow.

Adelaide was left standing in the entry hall, tears in her eyes. "Is it going to be all right, Millie?" she asked.

"I hope so, dear," Millie said. "Now go find your father."

A half an hour later Millie found the girl sobbing in her room, inconsolable at the news that she would not be visiting her cousins Zillah and Adah in Pleasant Plains. "I know why Mother doesn't like Elsie," Adelaide cried. "She ruins everything! Mother has left me, and now Father is leaving me, too. All because of her!"

"May I sit down beside you?" Millie asked.

"Yes," Adelaide said, "if you give me a handkerchief and don't look at my red nose."

"You must not blame little Elsie," Millie said. "She can't help it, you see. Let me tell you a story." Millie put her arm around Adelaide as she told the story of Cousin Horace meeting the beautiful young heiress Elsie Grayson in New Orleans. "Elsie was an orphan, too," Millie explained, "and Horace loved her very much. He believed she was the great love of his life. He wanted to take care of her, and so they were secretly married. They lived happily as man and wife for just a few months, until the marriage was discovered. Elsie's guardian came and took her away."

Millie carefully did not mention Uncle Horace's part in this, Adelaide having heard her father criticized once already this afternoon. "Cousin Horace was sure he would see his young wife again — as soon as he turned twenty-one, he could go and find her. But his Elsie died shortly after giving birth to their little girl. The baby was named Elsie, for her mother. Horace went to Europe to try to mend his broken heart, so the poor little girl has never known the love of her mother or her father. Now she must travel to a strange place, away from everything she knows. I know she will need a friend when she gets here."

Adelaide's eyes grew large as Millie talked. "It isn't her fault that Mother left me, really," she said.

"No," Millie agreed. "It isn't."

"I'll be her friend," Adelaide decided.

<hr />

Laylie was not much happier than Adelaide had been when Millie explained that they would be leaving for a place called Viamede in the morning, rather than Pleasant Plains.

"Is it north?" Laylie asked.

"No," Millie said, "it is south, almost as far as we can go. But I will be with you the whole way, and you will be with me. There and back." It was much harder sounding confident for Laylie's sake. *Whatever her mother's faults, Adelaide's future is assured. What will happen to Laylie when we return?* Millie was determined to speak to Uncle Horace before they set foot at Roselands again.

On the morning of their departure, their belongings were loaded aboard the Dinsmore's carriage, which would take them as far as Charleston. Uncle Horace had to speak with his own solicitor there, before proceeding overland to

Millie's Faithful Heart

Vicksburg on the Mississippi River. From Vicksburg they would journey by paddleboat to New Orleans to make arrangements in regard to the portion of Elsie's inheritance that lay in that city, and then proceed to Viamede.

The Dinsmore children were allowed to leave their lessons to bid their father farewell. Millie watched Uncle Horace shake hands with his sons and kiss his daughters, promising to bring them gifts and a new playmate when he returned.

Laylie was somber, knowing that they would travel through Charleston and very close to Meadshead, where Luke had died. Ajax, Uncle Horace's driver, seemed to understand, and took the girl under his wing. He offered to let her ride with him on the box, as the weather was fair. Laylie looked to Millie for approval, then scrambled up onto the seat beside him. Millie envied her the distraction. Charleston was also where Charles had gone, and between that and the proximity of Meadshead, Millie was not looking forward to their stay. She couldn't help but agree with Laylie that the carriage was headed the wrong direction when it turned out of Roselands.

"Now, now, you will enjoy Charleston," Uncle Horace said, as if reading Millie's thoughts from her somber expression. "I always have. She is the jewel of the South. Many of our finest families have built homes there. The society is marvelous."

"Isn't Charleston where you fought your duel, Uncle Horace?"

"Yes, and won the fair Isabel's heart. And if we meet nine-toed Judge Crockett, be sure to ask him about it. His story is less than accurate, but it is amusing. I have heard him tell it at parties several times. He attributes my marriage to his marksmanship. As the good judge remembers it, Isabel was in love with him, but took me out of pity after I received my serious wound in the duel."

"I thought it was nothing more than a flesh wound?" asked Millie.

"That is true, but a burn along the ribs is much more romantic than a missing toe. Judge Crockett is single to this day and blames it entirely on his limp."

Millie had almost forgotten the dry humor—he was never quite mirthful—of the uncle she had traveled with from Pleasant Plains. She found to her surprise that she had missed him, even though they were living in the same house. Roselands had somehow muffled him and made him seem less than he was or could be. *If he stays there long enough, will he disappear, leaving nothing but a handsome shell standing next to Aunt Isabel at parties and social functions?*

"I will remember to ask him," Millie smiled. "But surely we won't be there long enough for socializing."

"We will stay at the Breandan town home," Uncle Horace said. "My father-in-law is not only the publisher of the local paper, but they have one of the largest, most profitable plantations in the area."

"Uncle . . . for Laylie's sake I would rather not stay at the plantation. She is still much occupied with her brother's death."

"The Breandans live in their town home, a mansion really. As field hands, I'm sure Luke and Laylie never saw the place. It will hold no bad memories for her, and you will enjoy it immensely. Mrs. Breandan is a famous hostess, much like my Isabel."

The carriage route took them along the coast, first among tree-lined roads, then along the cliff top where

Millie's Faithful Heart

Millie could watch the gulls in the clear blue sky. The Dinsmore carriage was more comfortable than a stage-coach, but in the mid-afternoon a sudden acceleration in their speed, coupled with a wild swaying, caused Millie to grab the door handle just to stay in her seat.

"What on earth has gotten into Ajax?" Uncle Horace exclaimed. "Has he fallen asleep at the reins?"

Millie could only shake her head and try not to laugh. Judging from the shapes on top of the carriage-shadow that raced along the ground just outside her window, Ajax was not at the reins at all. Laylie had persuaded him to let her drive.

The violent swaying and jouncing settled down to an occasional lurch, and they traveled on without incident until they stopped that evening at an inn at the top of a cliff over the sea. While Uncle Horace talked with two other planters he met in the parlor, Millie and Laylie walked down a steep path to the rocky beach below. The rising tide rushed and gurgled among the rocks, first throwing plumes of spray, then drawing back in lace-edged waves, only to rush at them again. The water was cold when Millie put her hands in it, but that did not deter Laylie. Millie only turned her back for a moment, and when she turned again the young girl was pulling her dress off over her head.

"Laylie! Put your dress back on this instant!" Millie glanced around quickly to make sure they were alone. "Ladies do not take off their clothes in public."

"I'm not a lady," Laylie said. "I'm a slave. And *we* take 'em off to go swimming. I've got dust all over from riding on top of the coach! Look," she grimaced. "It's in my teeth!"

"We will wash up in our room. I expect you to act like a lady, just as Zillah or Adah or Fan would."

Laylie reluctantly pulled her dress back down. "If ladies can't go swimming, I'm not sure I want to be one."

"They certainly *can* go swimming," Millie assured her. "They wear bathing suits."

"What's a bathing suit?"

Millie explained and promised to find a picture of one for the young girl, but Laylie shook her head. "Wearing clothes in the water is unnatural."

"Nonetheless, I will expect you to wear them. Let's walk farther down the beach." Laylie followed along as Millie led the way. They found a wonderful sandy spot and Millie picked up a stick and wrote *Millie Keith* in the damp sand.

"What's that say?" Laylie asked. "The letters are all curly."

"It's cursive writing," Millie explained, "Can't you read it?"

"It don't look much like letters," Laylie squinted.

Of course she can't read it. She never learned to write, just to read the typeset letters on the pages of books. "Would you like me to write your name?" Millie asked.

"No," Laylie said. "Write 'freedom.' I want to see what it looks like."

Millie wrote the word in large letters, giving them an extra flourish. "Do you remember when Old Rachel talked to you about freedom?" Millie asked, standing back to look at her work.

"And Jesus," Laylie said, glancing at her from under thick lashes.

"And Jesus," Millie agreed. "The Savior we read about in the Bible. Have you thought any more about Him?"

"You mean about being a Christian, like you?"

"Yes," Millie said, "about giving your life to Him. Remember how you said you hoped that Luke had stolen away to Jesus? Well, you can do that right now, Laylie. He wants to save you."

"I thought about it some," Laylie said. "About Jesus and sin. Especially about sin. I'm not good like you or Rachel. Even Luke was better than me. I steal, and sometimes I lie. Lately I've been lying more than I've been stealing," she said matter-of-factly, throwing a rock into the waves. "But . . . if I could hit Borse in the head with a rock, I surely would." This last was said with such passion that it gave Millie a chill. "Just like David hit Goliath! That's sin, like Rachel said. Just like you read in the Bible. Hateful sin, but I don't care. If I was God, and God was me, I wouldn't like Borse. "

"God knows you hate Borse," Millie said gently. "He knows what's in your heart, and He knows everything you have ever done. He still loves you, Laylie. Jesus died for you while you were still a sinner. That's what the Bible says. Remember? You can ask His forgiveness, and He can change your heart right now."

"If he can do all of the stuff in the Bible," Laylie said, "why is this old world such a rotten place?"

Lord, how do I explain this? "Laylie, do you remember who Satan is?"

"He's the bad guy that tricked Eve."

"He's the bad guy," Millie agreed. "Like . . . like wicked King John in *Robin Hood*. King John was just a pretender—he took the throne while the real king, good King Richard, was away. And he did all kinds of evil things. Well, Satan is just like that. He is a pretender who is doing evil things, and convincing men to do them, too." Millie took Laylie by the hand. "When Jesus, the real King, comes back, He is going to throw that pretender in prison and lock him up forever."

"Just like King John got thrown in prison," Laylie said.

"That's right. But until he is thrown in prison . . . the whole world is a little like Nottingham. There is an evil impostor trying to rule it. And we only have two choices. We can be on the side of the good king, or we can be on the side of the bad king. But if we are going to be on the side of the good king—on Jesus' side—then we can't serve the bad king. We can't keep on lying or stealing or hating. We have to let Jesus help us stop doing that, and serve Him with all our hearts."

"I wish the good king would hurry up and come back," Laylie said. "And throw Satan in hell and Borse with him."

"Laylie," Millie took her hand. "If King Jesus came back right now, which side would you be on? Would you be one of His good followers? Or would you be serving the impostor—just like Borse?"

Laylie's eyes grew big. "I . . . "

Just then a wave rushed at them, and Laylie pulled her hand from Millie's and ran up the beach. Millie lifted her skirts to keep them from getting wet, and followed.

"I want to go back now," Laylie said. "The ocean's coming up." When Millie looked back, all of her writing in the sand had washed away.

Millie and Uncle Horace had a marvelous supper of chowder and fresh bread with butter and preserves, and Uncle Horace had no objection when Millie suggested they make sure Ajax and Laylie, who were eating in the kitchen, had the same. As Millie was brushing her hair, she suddenly realized that she could write to her mother freely for the first time since she had arrived at Roselands. Aunt Isabel was not there to read the letter, and she could post it the next day.

She wrote long into the night, and often had to stop before her tears fell on the page and made the fresh ink run. She wrote about Laylie and Luke, about Aunt Isabel and the Dinsmore children, why she had not been more forthcoming in her letters, and how she was on her way to meet little Elsie. Finally, she turned to Charles Landreth.

"Mamma, pray for me," she wrote, after telling the whole story. "I know I failed God when I fell in love with Charles. My heart hurts so badly I sometimes have difficulty breathing. Why can't God just wash these feelings out of my heart—like the waves washed my words from the sand?"

It was wonderful to be able to put her true feelings on paper once more. She longed for her mother's advice, but knew no letter from home would follow her to Viamede.

"I love you all so much," Millie wrote. "And I cannot wait to come home. I feel so, so much older. Pray for me, and pray that I find some way to bring Laylie with me when I come, and that I find a way to lead her to Jesus. I know I don't need to tell you, but please be careful what you write. Isabel will read the letters before I do." Millie could write no more than one letter a day, and cried over each. In the following days she wrote to Aunt Wealthy and Rhoda Jane, explaining as much as she had to her mother, and asking for their prayers.

Charleston was even more beautiful than Philadelphia, but that could have had something to do with the explosion of blossoms in every garden. The tree-lined streets were cobbled and spacious; the homes and buildings the work of skilled architects and planners. The Breandan town home was a magnificent three-story brick affair towering above its quiet street, surrounded by lovely trees.

They were greeted warmly at the door by a round, bald man who was introduced as Isabel's father. His wife, an aged image of Isabel grown thinner and painted somewhat badly, stood at his side. The housekeeper took one look at Laylie and whisked her out of sight. Millie was more than a little worried about where she had been taken. Mrs. Breandan asked a maid to escort Millie to her room so that she could freshen up, and Millie was relieved to find Laylie there unpacking her toiletries.

"This is Terria, Millie," Laylie said, pointing to the housekeeper with a hairbrush she had just pulled from a bag. "She used to be in the kitchen at the big house at Meadshead."

"And you was always stealing food," the woman said, cuffing Laylie's ear. "What your brother would say if he knew you was in Charleston, I don't know. He thinks you're away safe at Roselands."

The hairbrush fell from Laylie's hand and clattered across the wooden floor. "Luke?"

"You got other brothers I don't know about?"

Laylie sat down suddenly and Millie knelt beside her. "We thought Luke was dead," she said, putting an arm around the girl.

"Most troublesome dead man I ever saw," Terria said. "He's run twice, but they drag him back. Borse can't beat him to death, starve him to death, or work him to death, though Lord knows he's tried. Yes, ma'am, I'd say he was alive."

CHAPTER

Too Good To
Be True

*Always give yourselves fully to
the work of the Lord, because
you know that your labor
in the Lord is not
in vain.*

1 CORINTHIANS 15:58

The next day dawned in pink and gold. Millie watched the sky lighten from her bed, not sure whether she had slept or not. She had spent much of the night talking and praying with Laylie, and trying to figure out how she could arrange a visit for Laylie with Luke. The time had come to speak to Uncle Horace about Laylie. She did not see how she could put it off any longer, and felt sure he would be sympathetic to a plea for Luke also. He had, after all, tried to buy the young man. The more Millie thought about it, the more sure she was that he would help her.

Laylie was still asleep when Millie went in search of her uncle. Unfortunately, when she found him, he was sitting with his father-in-law, deep in discussion.

"Ah, Millie!" Uncle Horace said when she entered. "Didn't I tell you she wouldn't be long abed?"

"You did," Mr. Breandan beamed. "I was just offering to conduct your uncle on a day of sightseeing," he waved a hand expansively as if showing a view before him. "My wife has a dinner party planned for this evening, but we will be home in plenty of time."

Uncle Horace nodded. "You will love the Charleston Museum. It is the oldest in the nation. Shall we leave right after breakfast?"

"That would be delightful," she said, smiling. Asking about Laylie would have to wait, but Uncle Horace seemed in a magnanimous mood this morning.

Millie found Terria in her room when she returned. The woman held onto Laylie, who was still in her nightgown, with one hand, and was trying to smack her with the other. But every time Terria swung her hand, Laylie managed to duck, and was doing her best to kick the woman's shins as well.

"Let her go this instant!" Millie commanded. "What on earth is going on here?"

"I found this child *sleeping*, miss," Terria said, giving up on smacking Laylie and giving her a shake instead. "Missus don't allow that kind of laziness in her house!"

"I said let her go! She had my permission to sleep," said Millie.

"You don't give permission in this house," Terria sniffed. "And the sooner I remind this child of that, the fewer licks she's gonna take."

"You may leave now," Millie said. "Laylie will help me dress." The woman sniffed again on her way out.

"Laylie, you must stay out of trouble today." Millie opened her trunk and chose a blue gown that compromised nicely between stunning and sensible; it seemed the appropriate thing to wear to a museum. "I'm going to ask Uncle Horace to buy Luke. He agreed last fall; surely he will agree again. I need you to be on your best behavior, do you understand?"

"Luke don't want to belong to Mr. Horace," Laylie said. "He wants to be free. I've got to see him today, Millie. He's not gonna know I'm here!"

"One thing at a time," Millie laughed. "Let's work on one thing at a time. I will figure out a way for you to see him. But you must promise to stay here and do every bit of work Terria gives you to do while I am gone."

"Trade promises," Laylie said. "I'll promise to stay out of trouble if you promise I can see Luke."

"I promise I will do everything in my power to help you see him," Millie said.

"And say 'amen,' " Laylie demanded.

"Amen?"

"When you really mean something you say to God, you always say 'amen.' "

"I will do everything in my power to help you see Luke, amen," Millie said.

"I will stay here till you get back, amen," Laylie said seriously.

Millie was humming to herself when she went downstairs to meet her uncle. For the first time in weeks, it seemed that everything was going to be all right.

✦

Charleston harbor sparkled in the sunshine, but soon Millie realized that the sparkle was inside of her, as it followed them from sunny morning into the dark halls of the museum. Mr. Breandan insisted that they have the full tour, including viewing the *Phoenix*, formerly known as the *Best Friend* of Charleston. The train was a primitive version of the one Millie had ridden on during her trip to Roselands, and there was indeed a flatcar piled high with bales of cotton between the engine and the passenger cars, just as the Colonel had said. Millie smiled, thinking of the old man writing himself into the story.

"What do you think of her?" Mr. Breandan asked.

"The engine is a good deal smaller than the one on the train we took from Pittsburgh to Philadelphia."

Mr. Breandan puffed up his cheeks. "The old *Phoenix* may not be the top of the line now, young lady, but she is due some respect. Not more than six years ago, she was the first and the best of her kind in the United States of

America. We in Charleston are quite proud of her still." He started to recount the tale of the explosion of the steam engine, but Uncle Horace stopped him. "I think we have heard that one," he said, winking at Millie.

They spent the rest of the day in pleasant sightseeing, returning in plenty of time to freshen up for the dinner party. Laylie had been as good as her 'amen.'

"I guess that child is learning something at Roselands after all," Terria said. "She's turning into a hard worker."

"Did you talk to your uncle yet?" Laylie asked as soon as they were alone.

"Not yet. I can't ask him in front of Mr. Breandan. Be patient."

"If I have to wait much longer to see Luke I'm gonna die," Laylie said.

"I will talk to him as soon as I can," Millie assured her.

The Honorable Judge Crockett was a special guest at Mrs. Breandan's dinner party that night. He was an odd little man with a huge head and smile that seemed to split it from ear to ear. His cummerbund was quite tight, his trousers quite loose, and his cravat tied in the most extravagant of styles. Millie was seated on his left, and Uncle Horace, much to his distress, on the gentleman's right. Millie bowed to pray before she began her meal as always.

"Did you drop something, my dear?" the judge inquired, lifting the edge of the snowy tablecloth to peer underneath.

"I was saying grace," Millie explained.

"Not necessary," he said with a laugh. "Mrs. Breandan's cook hasn't poisoned anyone this year!" He laughed at his own joke.

"He's up for re-election," the woman seated on Millie's left explained in a whisper. "The Breandans feel they owe him something, because of the tragedy, you know."

"What tragedy?" Millie whispered back a little too loudly, for Judge Crockett cleared his throat.

"I suppose Horace has told you his version of the duel," he said too loudly for Millie's comfort. "While it is true that he shot my toe half off . . . I could take off this boot and show you." Here he reached under the table for his boot, but mercifully it was too tight to come off easily.

"That won't be necessary," Mrs. Breandan said.

"What Horace hasn't mentioned, I am sure, is that if he hadn't maimed me, *I* would have married Isabel!"

"Really?" Millie could not imagine Isabel beside this man. "You must be terribly grieved by the loss."

"You cannot imagine. My entire life—my course of existence—was altered by the loss of that toe!"

"I meant by the loss of your love," Millie explained.

"Half of a toe," Uncle Horace muttered. "It was only half." Judge Crockett glared at him across the spring asparagus.

"I knew a man who lost his whole toe once, heroically, at Valley Forge," Millie said in an attempt to change the subject. "It froze and fell off." She realized her hostess was looking at her with horror from across the table, but Judge Crockett leaned closer to her.

"Was his life changed forever?" he asked.

"For the better, I believe," Millie said. "George Washington himself shook his hand!"

"And did he live to be a wealthy, famous man?"

"No. When he died, he owned only a small farm," she said.

Millie's Faithful Heart

"His death was a result of losing that toe, I have no doubt, no matter the span of years in between. People quite underestimate the importance of the pedal digits. And they cannot be overlooked in a political campaign. I cannot tell you the number of times my toe has become an issue," said Judge Crockett.

Uncle Horace rolled his eyes.

Mrs. Breandan elbowed her husband. "Speaking of issues," he said hastily, "what is the price of cotton going to do next year? I have heard some speculation . . . "

Millie was relieved to spend the rest of the evening eating quietly as plantation matters were discussed.

"I fear you might have spent a most boring evening," Uncle Horace said as he bade her goodnight, "if it were not for the fact that a wise person once told me that there is no one you cannot learn something from."

"That is true," Millie said. "I have learned at least one thing."

"And what is that?" he asked.

"That I do not enjoy Mr. Crockett's company."

Uncle Horace laughed heartily. "You are my favorite traveling companion, Millie Keith," he said.

"Since I am your favorite niece," Millie said. "May I speak to you about something?"

He bowed. "What do you wish?"

"Do you remember Luke?" she asked.

"Laylie's brother. I remember."

"He's not dead," said Millie.

"That's excellent news! And more timely than I can tell you. Borse must have assumed I was inquiring after another slave, and I can't tell you how glad I am to know the young man is alive." He cleared his throat uncomfortably, and then went on. "I know you have grown fond of Laylie. I have discussed purchasing her for you with my father-in-law. He will not part with her. In fact, he wants the child left at Meadshead on our return."

The air around Millie seemed to thicken until it was hard to breathe. "Uncle . . . Aunt Isabel sold Laylie to me in exchange for my entertaining at her parties. She hasn't provided the papers, but . . . "

Uncle Horace shook his head. "That is not possible," he said. "Isabel does not own Laylie. She belongs to Meadshead, as does her brother."

"She said they were part of her inheritance from her grandmother . . . "

"You must have misunderstood . . . " *Was there hesitation in his voice?* Millie wondered. "The property and slaves will go to her older brother George. I'm very sorry, Millie. There is not one thing Isabel or I can do about it, or rest assured we would. I had hoped to keep this from you until our return, but perhaps it is kinder this way. And the girl can look forward to seeing her brother. You have seen the Breandans," he said, almost apologetically. "You know they are not bad people."

"I have seen Borse, and I assure you he is," Millie said. "I believe he threatened Laylie's life."

"But we thought the boy was dead, did we not? And here we find that he is alive! Millie, I know your views on slavery. I believe they have shaded your perceptions of Borse. I am sure all will be well."

⌒

Millie walked through the darkened halls toward her room. All *will* be well? She could still hear Borse's words:

Millie's Faithful Heart

"That little gal is going to end up the same place as her brother—six feet deep. And it's me that's going to put her there." What will I tell Laylie? *Lord,* Millie prayed, *You can't let this happen! We need a miracle!* She pushed open the door to her room to find Laylie sitting up waiting for her.

"Luke ran," Laylie said.

"He what?" asked Millie.

"He heard that I was in town from Terria's man, Roz, and he ran. Borse is going to come here, Millie. I'm afraid."

"Why would you be afraid? He . . ." Millie noticed the lace curtain moving in the breeze. She was sure the window had been shut. "You can come out, Luke," Millie said quietly. "I know you are here."

"Come out," Laylie whispered. "She's not going to turn you in." Luke scooted out from under the bed.

Millie asked, "Does anyone know you are here?" Though her voice seemed steady, her mind was reeling.

"No, miss," he said. "Came up the tree and in the window. I had to see Laylie. She says she's goin' with you . . . to freedom. Says you's gonna set her free."

"Laylie . . ." Millie covered her mouth with her hands while she found the words. "Isabel lied to me. She told me she could sell you, but she could not. They are going to take you back to Meadshead when we return from Viamede. And there's nothing I can do to stop them."

"No!" Luke said, putting his arm around his little sister. "I'm not letting her go back to Meadshead. Borse has been waiting. This is our only chance, Laylie girl. You gotta go with me now."

Jesus, Millie prayed silently. *What do I do?* Suddenly she remembered Shiprah and Puah—the midwives Pharaoh commanded to kill the Hebrew babies. They did not obey his commands. They hid the babies and saved their lives.

"I don't know how we're gonna do it," Luke was saying. "Everybody round here knows Borse. They will watch the roads and fields. I've run before, but I didn't get far."

Be strong and courageous. "I know a way," Millie said. "I can get you far from here in one day, too far for Borse to follow. Laylie, get your things and put them in a bundle. And put on your cloak. You are going to take a train ride."

"They're not going to let us on any train," Luke said.

"You're not going to ask. Come on, we need to hurry," Millie said, gathering three or four hatboxes from her trunk.

"You coming with us?" Laylie asked, looking at Millie with wide eyes.

Millie turned to Luke. "Luke, do you know the way to the train?"

"No," Luke admitted. "I've never been to the train before."

"Well, I do. And what will people think if they see the two of you walking the streets alone at night?" Millie grabbed her own cloak and a parasol and moved to the window. "Come on!" Millie said in an urgent whisper.

Luke climbed out of the window first, stepping carefully out onto the branch. It sank under his weight, but sprang back up as he made his way to the trunk. Laylie followed him, carrying her bundle, and Luke lowered her to the ground and then jumped down after her. Millie tossed the hatboxes and her parasol out the window, and Laylie caught them one by one.

"Strong and courageous," Millie muttered as she gathered her skirts. "Strong and *very* courageous!" The branch sank under her weight as well, and she grabbed at the leafy branch above her with one hand, while she stretched to shut the window with the other. Then she crept to the trunk, groping her way in the semi-darkness, then sat on the branch and lowered her feet.

"Hang down by your hands," Luke said. "I'll catch you."

Millie managed to turn onto her stomach and push off the limb. Her fingers were slipping when she felt Luke's hands around her waist. He set her on the ground. "Thank you," she said, brushing herself off. "Now take a hatbox or two and follow me."

"Why are we carrying these hatboxes?" Laylie asked.

"So it will look like I have been shopping," said Millie.

"The shops are closed," Laylie pointed out. "Nobody else is shopping at this time of night."

"I'll pretend I am taking them to a sick friend, then," Millie said, feeling foolish and suddenly quite afraid. The moon was half full, and light enough to see the faces of the people on the street. She started toward the train station, but made an abrupt turn when she saw two people walking toward her.

She tried not to walk quickly. They walked several blocks and then Millie made another turn, then another. *Which way is the Phoenix?*

They had walked the streets for half an hour and Millie was beginning to despair. *Which way is the train? The harbor? The Breandan's home for that matter?* Luke and Laylie were depending on her, and she was completely turned around. *Be strong and courageous.* Suddenly a form stepped out of the shadows just ahead of them. Millie turned away, but not quickly enough.

"Millie? Millie Keith? What on earth are you doing here?" Charles Landreth stepped into the light. Otis was right behind him. Millie glanced over her shoulder, but

Luke and Laylie had disappeared. *Did Charles see them? Surely Otis did not.*

"Why, Millie! Yay! I am just so thrilled to see you," Otis said. "Charles was just saying . . ."

"I was just saying goodbye, Otis," Charles said. "And I will see you later."

"But . . ."

"Goodbye, Otis," said Charles.

"Goodbye," Otis said. Millie could have sworn his shoulders drooped as he walked away.

"Nice night for a stroll," Charles said, nodding to a couple they passed, and then when they were out of earshot, "I see you have been . . . shopping?"

"Shopping?" asked Millie.

"I saw your hat-bearing friends before they stepped into the alley," he said. "Are you in trouble, Millie?"

Millie stopped and looked up at him for a full minute, trying to decide. There simply was no choice. "Can I trust you, Charles?"

"With your life, I hope," he said. "Let's walk. You might as well come, too," he said as they passed the mouth of the alley. Luke and Laylie fell in behind them.

"I'm helping Luke and Laylie escape to freedom."

There was the slightest hesitation in his pace, and then he walked on. "When I said with your life, I thought I meant in a more figurative way. You could be put in jail if you are caught. Or worse."

"Are you going to turn us in? You will have to, because I am not taking them back," she said.

"So, Millie Keith is an abolitionist — and worse," Charles said musingly. "I knew that something had Isabel worried. An abolitionist is a very bad thing to be, you know. I doubt even Horace would approve, and he's quite fond of you."

"He does not approve," said Millie.

"He is with you here in Charleston, I presume. You must be staying with the Breandans. Does he know you are out walking about tonight? No, of course not. He would never allow a lady out alone."

"You have asked enough questions, Charles, and don't seem to need my help answering them. Are you going to help me or turn me in?"

"Help you, of course, and no one will ever hear a word of it from me. You have my word as a gentleman and a Landreth. We make gruesome ancestors, but the family pride is a great motivator for keeping promises. Where are we going? Are you planning to walk all the way to the Mason-Dixon line?"

"To the *Phoenix*," Millie said. "I think I can get them out of town and far away before anyone knows they are gone."

"We are a bit turned around, then," Charles said, redirecting her steps. They had wandered quite a distance, as it took half an hour to find the train yard.

The *Phoenix* lay quiet on the tracks, a ghost train in the pale moonlight.

"You have purchased their tickets, I presume?"

Millie walked over to the train and pulled on a bale of cotton.

"Those are heavy," Charles said, looking at Luke. "Aren't you going to help her?"

"Charles!" Millie said, exasperated.

"Oh, all right," Charles said, jumping to help Luke. Together they began pulling cotton bales out from the bottom of the stack until they could rearrange the bales to make a cave in the center, just big enough for Luke and Laylie to slide into, with enough space above them for air to flow in.

"They's gonna see these extras," Luke pointed out. "Less'n we move them." He swung one up onto his shoulder. Charles followed his lead, and the six bales they had removed were soon hidden down an alleyway.

"They will notice them eventually, I expect," Charles said. "But it will take some time. You are going to have to stay in here all night and most of tomorrow," Charles said. "When the train stops, you'll have to kick your way out, and hope no one is watching when you do."

Luke picked up Laylie and started to slip her into the cave, but she wiggled from his arms and ran to Millie.

"Millie," she said. "Did something ever happen to you that was so good that you couldn't believe it really happened?"

"Yes," Millie said. "I think it has."

"I think something that good . . . it's got to be from King Jesus. I want to be on His side. Will you show me how?"

"All right," Millie said.

"What are you gonna do?" Luke asked.

"Pray," Laylie told him.

Millie explained to Luke, "The Bible says, 'If you confess with your mouth, "Jesus is Lord," and believe in your heart that God raised him from the dead, you will be saved. For it is with your heart that you believe and are justified, and it is with your mouth that you confess and are saved.' Laylie is about to get saved," said Millie, smiling into Laylie's eyes.

"She don't need savin'," Luke said. "She needs to get on that train."

"Now don't be hasty," Charles said. "The lady has gone through a great deal of trouble for you tonight. Give her a moment." Charles then encircled them in his arms and nudged them to the side until they were between the two railcars, out of plain sight to any passersby.

"Best to try and conceal ourselves a little," Charles said to Millie.

"Thank you," Millie said hurriedly. She felt very awkward with Charles and Luke watching, but she took a deep breath and began. "Laylie, do you believe that Jesus is Lord and that you are a sinner who needs a Savior?"

"I do, I really do!" Laylie said, nodding her head.

"Then you need to ask Jesus to forgive your sins," said Millie, casting a quick glance beyond the railcar to be sure the four of them were still alone.

"Jesus," Laylie prayed, closing her eyes in obvious imitation of the way she had seen Millie pray so often. "Forgive my evil heart. I'm tired of Satan, and I don't want anything to do with him anymore. I don't want to hate or steal or lie. Millie says You died on a cross to take my sins away, and I *want* you to have them. I want You to be my King Jesus from now on, amen."

Millie opened her eyes. Tears glittered on Laylie's cheeks. "Millie!" she said in amazement. "It worked! I don't want to hit Borse with a rock anymore!"

"You get in that hole," Luke said, picking her up.

"Tell them about me, Millie," she said as she scrambled in. "Tell Zillah and Adah and Fan. Tell that Damaris Drybread I liked what she did with that hat."

"I'll tell her," Millie promised. "And I will tell them to pray for you every single day. I'm going to miss you so much!"

Luke followed his sister into the hole and Millie handed in their bundles. Charles put the last bale back in place, and they were hidden.

"May I walk you home, Miss Keith?" He offered his arm, but Millie looked in dismay at her hatboxes. Charles laughed as he helped her gather them up. They walked through the streets together to the Breandan home.

"How did you get out?" Charles asked. "I assume you didn't just inform them you were going for a stroll." Millie pointed up to the tree.

"Would you like a boost, m'lady?" Charles made his hands into a stirrup. Millie hesitated for only a second before she slipped her muddy boot into his hands.

"Don't worry, I'll close my eyes," he said. He boosted her straight up, as if she weighed less than Laylie. Millie caught the branch and managed to pull herself up. She held on tightly as she edged toward the window.

"Do you need any help?" Charles asked.

"No," Millie said, stretching to catch the sash with the toe of her boot. She managed to raise the sash, and taking hold of the leafy branch above her, edged toward the window. The branch sank as she worked her way out, the result being that the windowsill was at her waist when she finally reached it. She let go of the branch and managed to topple gracefully in, head first.

"Are you all right?" Charles called in a loud whisper.

"Of course," Millie whispered back. "Why wouldn't I be?"

Charles tossed up the hatboxes one by one, and Millie caught them and pulled them inside. As she put the last one safely in the corner of her room, she turned back to the window, saying "Thank you, Charles, for—ahhhh!" Charles was perched on the tree limb, leaning on the windowsill.

"You are a thief, Millie Keith," he said. "You've stolen my heart, and there is just nothing I can do about it. When can I see you again?"

Millie's Faithful Heart

"We are leaving tomorrow," Millie said, "but this may cause a commotion."

"If you are found out," Charles said, "should I break you out of jail, or confess so that they will lock us up together?"

Millie sighed. "Goodbye, Charles Landreth. And thank you again," she said, closing the window quickly—as if that would prevent her heart from melting like butter. Millie felt the blush burning in her cheeks as she watched Charles walk away. Then she got down on her knees beside her bed and closed her eyes.

Lord Jesus . . . Millie paused to settle her thoughts. *Thank You for protecting Luke and Laylie tonight. Please continue to protect them and provide for them. Guide them safely to freedom. Let Luke know that it was "for freedom that Christ has set us free," and that he will only be truly free when he gives his life to You. Thank You so much for letting me lead Laylie in her prayer tonight. I know all of the angels in heaven are rejoicing with me. It was really hard to do in front of Luke and Charles, and I thank You for giving me courage. And speaking of Charles . . . You know what is in my heart. I am so thankful You sent him to help us tonight. I know You have him in my life for a reason. It is hard, Lord. But I trust You with my heart where he is concerned. Help me to always be faithful to You.* Millie opened her eyes and looked up. Then she sighed and said, *But he is a little wonderful, isn't he?*

Between trying not to think of Charles smiling at her in the moonlight, thanking God for Laylie's salvation, and praying that they would reach freedom safely, Millie didn't sleep a wink that night.

CHAPTER

11

Wonderful Watchman

The Lord will keep you from all harm — he will watch over your life; the Lord will watch over your coming and going both now and forevermore.

PSALM 121:7–8

he next morning Millie ignored Laylie's absence as long as possible, taking extra time to brush her hair and dress herself. *What will I say to Uncle Horace?* She was saved from making the announcement by the arrival of Borse with the news that Luke had run away.

"Have you seen Laylie this morning?" Uncle Horace asked Millie.

"I have not," she said, painfully aware that a blush was creeping up her neck.

"I saw her," Terria said, and Millie's heart almost stopped. "Dawdling around in the kitchen no mor'n an hour ago." *Did Laylie come back?* Millie searched the woman's face. She certainly looked as if she was telling the truth.

Mr. Breandan ordered a search for the girl, and the house slaves all joined in. An upstairs maid found a locked door, and there was much pounding and calling, demanding that the girl come out before the key was found and the room proved empty. Charles Landreth appeared in the midst of the chaos.

"I heard you were in town, sir," he said, shaking hands with Uncle Horace. "And thought I would pay my regards." He turned and bowed formally to Millie. "And what is causing this commotion?"

"Laylie is missing," Millie explained. "And her brother Luke has run away from Meadshead."

"Why can't these people simply stay where you put them?" Mrs. Breandan asked, wringing her hands.

"Ummm . . . yes. Where you put them. I quite agree," Charles said. "Horace, I was wondering if I might take your niece for a walk? Surely she can be of no help here, and there is something I would like to speak to her about." Uncle Horace looked surprised, then glanced at Millie.

"Just a stroll down to the *Phoenix*," he said. "It's not far, and I know you are fascinated by technological progress. She will be starting her run in half an hour — just enough time to walk there, if we hurry."

"We viewed the train yesterday morning," Mr. Breandan said. "I have given the young lady a complete tour."

"I . . . I wouldn't mind seeing it once more before I leave," Millie said. She knew she was blushing furiously, but couldn't help it.

"Really?" Uncle Horace said, looking from Millie to Charles. "I am delighted! Delighted! One hour, Charles," he said. "We will be leaving as soon as the child is found."

Charles offered his arm when they reached the street. "You are horrible, Charles Landreth," Millie said. Charles stopped.

"Does that mean you wish to go back?" he asked teasingly.

"No, of course not. Hurry up or we will miss it!" she exclaimed, tugging at his arm and practically dragging him down the street.

Puffs of steam and smoke were belching from the engine when they arrived.

Millie examined the cotton bales, looking for telltale signs, but saw nothing. "Are they still there? Terria said she saw Laylie in the kitchen this morning."

"They are still in the cotton," Charles said reassuringly. "Terria was creating a rabbit's trail."

"How can you know for certain?" she asked.

"I have been here all night watching over your little Robin Hood," he said simply. Millie looked at him in surprise, but before she could say a word, the train started forward with a hiss and belch of steam, picking up speed quickly. She waved, and passengers, laughing, waved back.

"Now explain to me what you are doing in Charleston?" Charles tucked her hand under his arm as they started back to the Breandans. "I believed you to be on your way home to Pleasant Plains. You can't imagine my shock at finding you wandering the streets in the wee hours of the morning."

Millie explained about Elsie and the estate, and her delayed trip. They stopped outside the Breandan's front door. "Thank you, Charles, for your kindness," Millie said. "You really are a wonderful person."

"Make up your mind, Miss Keith," he said with a smile. "Am I horrible or wonderful? It would be awfully nice if you had decided by the time you return to Roselands. It would be even nicer if you decided to accept my proposal."

"Charles, I can never . . . "

"Shhhhh." He put a finger to her lips. "That's the wrong answer again. Just think about it until you return. I'll wait, just in case the answer changes." He opened the door and waved her inside. As soon as Charles had said his farewells, Millie went to her room. She shut the door and leaned against it. Putting a Scripture in her pocket was not going to help this time. When God searched her heart, He would find that she was in love with Charles, and there was not much she could do about it.

The search for Laylie proved fruitless, and by noon, Uncle Horace was sure she had gone with her brother.

"It's very hard on you, niece," Uncle Horace said. "But under the circumstances, I would not feel comfortable taking the child with us when she is returned. We would have to watch her constantly. Perhaps Mrs. Breandan can provide another servant for the remainder of the journey?"

Millie assured him that no servant was necessary. She was used to caring for herself on the frontier, and would be doing so again soon. Ajax had been sent back to Roselands, as they were taking the stagecoach cross-country to the Mississippi.

For the first week Millie prayed for Laylie and Luke almost without ceasing. They were so constantly on her mind that she feared she would say the wrong thing and give herself away, and she wasn't the only one involved now. Charles Landreth was not leaving for Pleasant Plains in just a few weeks. His home was in the South, and if word ever leaked out that he had helped slaves escape, it would do him great harm. *Lord*, Millie prayed. *Don't let me ever bring harm to Charles. No matter what.*

The long stagecoach ride across South Carolina, Georgia, Alabama, and Mississippi gave Millie a chance to see more of the South than she had ever imagined. At Roselands she met only the wealthy landowners that the Dinsmores considered their social equals. But in the crowded stagecoaches and roadside inns, she met people of every sort—small farmers who worked the land themselves, shopkeepers, tradesmen, and even free blacks who chose to stay in the South.

Uncle Horace was an excellent traveling companion, full of information on the history of towns they passed. When they reached Vicksburg, on the banks of the muddy Mississippi, they boarded *The River Lady*, a huge paddleboat. It was an elaborate affair with four decks, grand staircases, carpeted lounges, and spacious passenger cabins.

Wonderful Watchman

Millie was settled into the most luxurious room she had ever occupied, with plush carpets and rich furnishings. Uncle Horace warned her against the saloons and lounges on the top deck where gamblers played at games of chance.

At first glance the boat had looked like a floating cake, or perhaps a fairyland festival gliding down the river. But now that Millie was aboard, she could see that it was nothing like the neat and well-built cutter on which she had sailed across Lake Michigan, or the ship that had carried her down the coast from Philadelphia to Roselands. In fact, under her paint and facade, the *Lady* was a conglomeration of wood, tin, shingles, canvas, and twine. The scrollwork, carpets, and chandeliers looked as if they cost more than the boat itself.

"Quite true," Uncle Horace said when she voiced her observation. "Riverboats have such frequent accidents that investing a great deal of money in them would be unwise. Ten or more are lost each year on this river, depending on the water level."

They watched the linesman drop a rope with a weight on the end into the water from the bow of the ship, feeding out rope until the weight touched bottom. Uncle Horace explained that each knot was six feet, or one fathom from the next, and by counting how many passed through his hands, the linesman was able to estimate the depth of the murky water, a necessity with the constantly shifting sand bars.

His point was made clear the next day as Millie stood watching the massive paddle wheel. Uncle Horace was reading in a deck chair not ten feet away, but Millie had set aside her own book for the moment. A curly-headed baby boy of two, perhaps two and a half, toddled up to her and pointed, fascinated at the great wheel.

Millie's Faithful Heart

"Where did you come from?" Millie asked in surprise.

"Sammy," his mother called, "come back here!" An older brother appeared and dragged the reluctant toddler away. A few moments later he was back, tugging on Millie's skirt.

"You little rascal!" Millie said. "Did you escape again?"

"Dat dat dat!" the toddler exclaimed, pointing at the wheel and stamping his little feet in excitement.

" 'Dat' is a paddle wheel," Millie said, looking around for the child's mother. She was nowhere to be seen. "And you are going back to your parents." She picked the small boy up. Suddenly the boat lurched, throwing Millie hard against the rail. She grasped it frantically with her free hand and held onto the baby with her other. Passengers screamed, and Millie saw that some had been thrown to the deck by the impact.

Uncle Horace was at her side almost instantly, leading her away from the rail. Millie wrapped both arms around Sammy. *Thank You, Jesus*, she prayed. *If I had not picked him up when I did, he surely would have been thrown overboard, directly into the churning paddles.* There was a terrible rasping sound, a second lurch, and the *Lady* turned sideways in the current, then righted.

"What's the mark?" the pilot called from the back of the boat, asking the linesman at the bow to check the water's depth.

"By the mark, twain!" the linesman called back.

"That means the water's two fathoms—twelve feet—deep," Uncle Horace said. "We hit a sand bar, but we haven't run aground."

Suddenly the baby's mother rushed down the stairs, her husband at her side.

"Sammy, you naughty boy!" she scolded, taking the child from Millie's arms. "Thank you, miss. I was so frightened. I can't take my eyes off this one for an instant! We are going back to the cabin, and we are staying there."

The little boy smiled impishly at Millie over his mother's shoulder as she started back toward the stairs, and Millie waved. "I am never traveling by river with the children again, John Clemens," the poor woman was saying as they disappeared. "Don't even *think* of asking me . . ."

"Did anyone ever tell you that you lead a more exciting life than most young ladies?" Uncle Horace asked when they were sure there had been no damage to the hull. "Passengers spontaneously combust on trains or are tossed about like bowling pins on boats. Remind me never to travel with you by hot air balloon."

"I believe it is the Stanhope in me," Millie said, thinking that it was a good thing he didn't know exactly how exciting her life had been recently.

"It is the only explanation," Uncle Horace replied. "Dinsmores are far more restrained."

Spring had settled over the South. Somewhere Luke and Laylie were making their way north by night, following the stars. In Pleasant Plains, Damaris Drybread had said "I do" to Nicholas Ransquate. Millie smiled, thinking of the reception her mother had surely held for the newlyweds. Damaris would have insisted on sewing her own marriage quilt, of course, but the ladies would have made her rugs and curtains, tablecloths and napkins. They would have surrounded the couple with laughter and prayers that their future would be happy and blessed. And somewhere, Charles was . . .

Only the greatest exertion of willpower kept Millie from banging her head on the wall. *Lord, I don't want to think about him a million times a day!*

"You have changed, Millie Keith." Millie jumped at the sound of her uncle's voice. "I have never known you to be so quiet."

"I think I may have grown up, Uncle Horace," Millie said.

"Falling in love can have that effect," he said, gazing out over the water. "I am delighted that you and Charles are speaking again. I cannot help but feel that you were making a grave mistake, and now you have a second chance. Finding someone to love is not as easy as it appears in romantic books. I want both of you to be happy."

"Are you happy in your marriage, Uncle Horace?"

"I love Isabel," he said.

"Yes, but are you happy?" she asked.

"I think I could be, if . . . "

Millie waited, but he didn't finish the sentence. "Then perhaps love is not all that is necessary for happiness," Millie said softly.

"Perhaps you have grown up," he said, and they walked on in silence.

Millie spent time talking with the passengers and was able to practice her French more and more as they neared New Orleans. The words were not the only thing that changed. The food was rich with spices, peppers, and sauces that burned her mouth, but were delicious just the same.

They remained in New Orleans for a week, Uncle Horace being engaged in making the necessary arrangements in regard to that portion of little Elsie's inheritance which lay in the Crescent City. He was stunned to learn the true size of Elsie's estate. "Her guardian was certainly faithful to his trust," he commented, "and apparently very shrewd in making investments. During the child's minority, Horace Jr. will control a princely income."

"Do you regret his marriage less, then?" Millie asked.

"No. It will always be a mark on the Dinsmore name. Money can never make up for breeding."

When Uncle Horace's business was concluded, they boarded another paddleboat, not as grand as the *Lady*, but with huge windows in each stateroom from which to observe the passing scenery.

Teche Bayou reminded Millie of her own wild Kankakee Marsh and made her long for home. She spent time on the deck watching for ibis, egrets, and great herons, as well as the common birds that she would see in her beloved Kankakee, such as the jewel-like hummingbird that visited her hat one day looking for a meal among the silk flowers.

Her favorite was Hannibal, a brown pelican that had been adopted by the boat's captain. The bird was quite tame, flying alongside them, fishing for his breakfast or begging for scraps. When he caught a fish, he opened his mouth and turned his head down to let the water run out, making puddles on the deck. He would then tip his head back, swallowing the fish. One day Millie saw a saucy seagull swoop down and scoop Hannibal's breakfast from his open beak. Her sketchbook was soon filled with studies of the bird, which liked to sit on the deck in the afternoon sun.

The banks were teaming with life, above and below the water. The bulb-like eyes and long, toothy snouts of alligators broke the water's smooth surface, and Millie often saw the giant beasts basking in the sun. In the very early morning, when the boat was almost silent, she could hear their breath hiss like dragons as they rose from the depths. At night their eyes glowed like red sparks on the water, reflecting the lanterns on the deck.

The people of the bayou navigated the waters in canoes or rafts, and more than once Millie saw an alligator's nose clubbed to keep it away. Baby alligators sometimes sunned on the backs of their elders as they floated half-submerged. It was a different world than the marsh in Pleasant Plains, but it was impossible for Millie to see the bayou shrouded in morning mist and not feel like shouting praises to the Lord. When she walked on the deck alone, praying, or sat still reading her Bible, God's presence surrounded her, and for a few moments her heart would be free of its ache. She would keep to the deck until an evening mist rose off the water and the peep frogs and shiver owls began their night calls.

Now and again the trees and swamp subsided, giving way to cultivated fields, and the lordly villas of the plantation owners could be seen, shaded by magnificent oaks and magnolias. All had their own piers for the steamships to land and deposit or pick up goods, and many had sugar-houses or orange groves near the pier, evidence of their productivity. Often there were long rows of low cabins—the homes of the laborers. They did not seem as substantial as the cabins at Roselands, often having only rags for windows and doors, and the workers themselves were not as well-clothed, but Uncle Horace pointed out that the climate was much warmer.

One day they came in sight of a sugar and orange plantation with more fields than any they had passed before.

Wonderful Watchman

They swept by a large sugarhouse. Next came an immense orange orchard, and then a long and wide stretch of lawn — a lovely carpet of velvety green — and the most magnificent shade trees Millie had ever seen, half-concealing a colonnaded mansion.

"Viamede, the old Grayson place," the captain called.

"It seems the affairs here have been handled as well as those in New Orleans," Uncle Horace said as the boat rounded to the little pier.

Close by, in the shade of a great oak, stood an elderly slave woman with a child in her arms.

CHAPTER

Little Elsie

"See that you do not look down on one of these little ones. For I tell you that their angels in heaven always see the face of my Father in heaven."

Matthew 18:10

Little Elsie

The little girl wiggled with delight in her nursemaid's arms as the travelers stepped ashore. The woman set the child down as they approached. She was a beautiful child with hazel eyes and dark brown curls which looked golden brown in the sunlight. Millie smiled at her, and the little one smiled back for just a moment before her eyes went to Uncle Horace's face hopefully. He didn't seem to notice, but spoke to the nursemaid instead.

"You are Aunt Chloe, I assume?" he said.

"Yes, Master," she said, bowing her head.

"What's your name, child?" Uncle Horace addressed the girl at last.

"Elsie Dinsmore," she answered, with a small curtsey. "Are you my . . . " she wrinkled her brow, as if searching for the word, " . . . Grandpa?"

Uncle Horace knelt before her and they examined each other solemnly. "I believe I am," he said at last. "What do you think about that?"

Elsie considered him for a moment, and then her smile peeked out again. She threw both arms about his neck and gave him a kiss. Millie hid her own smile as Uncle Horace disengaged himself rather hastily and stepped back, wiping off the kiss with his handkerchief and looking as if he couldn't think of a thing to say.

"Aunt Chloe," Elsie whispered loudly, "why did Grandpa wipe my kiss off?"

"Don't whisper, child," Aunt Chloe said. "It's not polite."

"I am your cousin Millie," Millie said. "You don't know me, but I have been praying for you for years. May I have a hug?" Elsie jumped into her arms and Millie swung the little girl around until she giggled. Then she put her down gently.

"Welcome to Viamede, miss. Welcome, Master Dinsmore." Aunt Chloe made a curtsey to each.

A white woman and several servants came hurrying toward them across the lawn. The woman introduced herself as Mrs. Murray, the housekeeper. Her thick Scottish brogue spoke of a girlhood in Scotland, and her voice was beautiful and deep. There were more curtseys and welcomes. Slaves were assigned the task of carrying the luggage to the house, while the travelers, Mrs. Murray, Aunt Chloe, and Elsie followed at a more leisurely pace.

Uncle Horace was examining everything around him, from the buildings to the servants, but Millie smiled at little Elsie, who was walking by her nursemaid's side. Elsie smiled back, ran to her, and slipped a tiny hand into Millie's.

"Elsie is wonderful, Uncle Horace," Millie said at the first opportunity to do so without being overheard. "And her manners are quite nice. You won't need to worry a bit about taking her home to your family." They were standing on the veranda admiring the view as the boat that had brought them continued up the river.

"She's not a Dinsmore," Uncle Horace said. "Not a trace of Horace's looks about her. She must be all Grayson."

"Don't pretend you can harden your heart against her," Millie said. "I know you too well to believe it. I think Horace Jr. would be proud of his daughter if he could know her. She seems to be both sweet and intelligent."

Mrs. Murray arrived to announce that their apartments were ready and that their luggage had been disposed of.

Little Elsie

Aunt Chloe and Elsie showed Millie the way to her rooms, and waited as Millie changed into a dinner dress.

"Isn't my cousin pretty, Aunt Chloe?" asked Elsie.

Millie heard and laughed. "Thank you," she said to Elsie. "Would you walk with me to the dining room?" The little girl nodded and took her hand. "You are very pretty, too," Millie said in a whisper. "But there is something much more important than being pretty outside. Do you know what it is?"

"Jesus in my heart," the little girl said with a skip.

"Why, Elsie Dinsmore! How did you know that?" asked Millie.

"Aunt Chloe said so, and Mrs. Murray, too," the girl explained.

The travelers were summoned to the dinner table, and little Elsie, after climbing into her chair, folded her tiny hands and then peeked up at Uncle Horace through her lashes.

"Close your eyes, Grandpa," she said, and waited until he did before she murmured a short prayer of thanks for their food. Millie was delighted, but Uncle Horace fidgeted with his napkin and looked uncomfortable.

"She seems a well-behaved child," he said at last, as if she wasn't present.

"Yes," Elsie agreed, sounding very much like an adult. "I am very well-behaved."

"I see," Uncle Horace said, raising his eyebrows. "And how old are you, miss? Can you tell?"

"Four," the little girl said, holding up three fingers. "And Aunt Chloe says I'm too big to be naughty."

"Aunt Chloe is quite right," Uncle Horace said. "I should expect you to be good all of the time. Surely you were never naughty?"

"Yes, I was," she assured him, "when I was a baby. Aunt Chloe put me in the corner sometimes."

"And now that you are all grown up, what would Aunt Chloe do?" he asked.

"She would say 'Jesus is not pleased with my darlin' child when she's naughty,' " said little Elsie.

"And you care what Jesus thinks?" he asked curiously.

She looked at him with wide eyes. " Course I do!" she said.

Uncle Horace shook his head, but Millie smiled, thinking of the many prayers she had prayed for this little girl. Aunt Wealthy had been praying, too, as well as her parents. Elsie would delight them.

"She's been left with servants and they're making a hypocrite of her," Uncle Horace said to Millie when they had retired to the drawing room. "She is far too young to understand religion."

"She doesn't have to understand religion to learn about God," said Millie, taking a seat. "Only love. How old was Adelaide when she first knew you were her father and that you loved her?"

"That's entirely different!" said Uncle Horace defensively.

"Is it? At any rate, you must admit that her manners are amazing for a child of her age. She handles knife, fork, and spoon quite well, and seems gentle and refined in all she does."

"Yes," he said. "Evidence that she is Horace's child after all."

Millie could not help but think of Arthur, whose manners were no better than they had to be. Surely it was a matter of training, not heredity. Someone had loved this little girl enough to teach her well.

"I wish Cousin Horace could see her," Millie said. "I am sure he would be proud to be her father."

"You seem quite charmed with her. She is a pretty child, and perhaps that will reconcile Isabel to her presence."

"Ah-ha!" Millie said. "She has graduated from a creature to a child!"

"This is a fine old mansion," he said, changing the subject, "and seems well-furnished throughout. Shall we explore it?"

Millie was glad to agree, but they had not seen more than three rooms when they came upon an extensive library. There were valuable and rare books, works in every branch of literature, and Millie regretted that she would have so little time to enjoy them. There were also some fine paintings and beautiful pieces of statuary scattered through the house, the drawing room being especially rich in them.

They lingered for some time over these works of art, and then went out upon the veranda. From there they wandered to the lawn, where they strolled about a little, finally seating themselves under a beautiful magnolia tree.

"Is it possible, Uncle Horace," Millie asked, "that the Graysons were not as unrefined as you assumed? You have expressed nothing but delight with everything you have seen."

"No one could argue with their taste, perhaps. But still, they had no breeding," he said.

"What would it take to change your mind?" asked Millie.

"Discovering that they were royalty in hiding would certainly make my task with Isabel easier," he suggested. "But I had their background thoroughly checked when I discovered the marriage, and that is not the case."

"I wish I'd brought my sketchbook out with me!" Millie pointed toward a tree in whose shade Aunt Chloe was seated upon the grass with little Elsie in her lap, both busy with the flowers they had been gathering. "They make a beautiful picture. You won't separate them, will you, Uncle Horace? The child seems very fond of her nurse."

"Of course not! Jonati has her hands full with my own children. Elsie might as well have her own nursemaid."

At that moment little Elsie came running up with a flower in each hand.

"One for Grandpa, and one for Cousin Millie." She gave a graceful little curtsey as she presented them.

"Thank you, dear. They are very pretty," Millie said.

"What do I do with it?" Uncle Horace asked, holding the flower in two fingers.

"Put it in your buttonhole," said Elsie. "That's what Uncle does."

"Uncle? You have never met your uncles."

"Master Cameron, sir," explained Aunt Chloe, coming up. "He always told her to call him that."

Uncle Horace looked seriously at Elsie. "You mustn't call that man 'uncle' again. He was no relation to you. You come from a very important family on your father's side, and you must learn your place in society. You are a Dinsmore, and Dinsmores do not have common uncles."

Elsie drew back to the shelter of Aunt Chloe's arms, her eyes full of tears.

"There, there," Uncle Horace said more gently. "Don't cry. I'm not angry with you. You didn't know any better, and you will soon learn."

"Somebody's tired," Aunt Chloe said, gathering the child up. "I believe it's time for a nap, if you don't mind, Master Dinsmore."

"You are quite right, Aunt Chloe. A nap would help my disposition. I get quite irritable at this time in the afternoon," Uncle Horace said.

Both Aunt Chloe and Elsie looked at him uncertainly.

"By all means, take the child to bed," he said. "Do you ever feel that no one understands you?" he asked Millie, as the girl and her nursemaid hurried toward the house.

"A smile might help," Millie suggested. "It can be a subtle hint that one is making a joke or feeling friendly. I have found that smiles are quite helpful when speaking with children."

Uncle Horace stretched his lips. "It feels unnatural," he said. "Your face seems to settle naturally into a smile. But mine isn't meant for it."

"Nonsense!" Millie said, although he did look almost frightening. "It's like riding a horse. You feel awkward at first, but soon it will become second nature."

"Speaking of riding," Uncle Horace allowed his face to collapse into its natural somber state. "I hear there are fine saddle horses in the stables," he said. "If I order two of them brought round, will you ride over the plantation with me?"

"Gladly! I have been missing my rides."

They returned from their ride even more impressed with Viamede's beauty and with the abilities of the friends and servants who had been charged with the plantation's upkeep.

After tea, while Uncle Horace was behind closed doors with the overseer, Millie stopped on the veranda to chat with Mrs. Murray. The evening air was soft, and fireflies rose from the lawn flashing golden messages to the night. Mrs. Murray's talk soon turned to the Grayson family, particularly Horace Jr.'s wife—the first Elsie.

Millie's Faithful Heart

"She was very lovely," Mrs. Murray said, "both in person and in character—a sweet, earnest, childlike Christian. The wee bairn is wonderfully like her mother. She seemed to me a lamb of the fold from her very birth—no doubt in answer to the mother's prayers. You know, Miss Keith, that she lived scarce a week after her babe was born. All her anxiety was that little Elsie should be trained up in the nurture and admonition of the Lord. Her constant prayer was that He would be pleased to make her His own. The wee bairn isn't perfect, of course, but quite as near it as grown folk. It's evident that she loves our blessed Savior." The old lady brushed away a tear. "Mr. Cameron used to fret that she was too good to live, like her mother before her. But I can't think that early piety is any sign that life will be short—except, of course, when God's work of grace is fully done. She comes from God-fearing blood, Miss Keith, and the Lord's faithful to His promises, showing mercy to thousands of generations of them that love Him and keep His commandments."

Just then, Mrs. Murray was called away to her duties and Millie stood alone, thinking about the first Elsie—Elsie Grayson—how the choices she had made still echoed in the hearts of those who loved her, even after her death. *What about the choices I have made and am still to make?*

Viamede is a paradise, Mamma. Being here is a bit like walking through a storybook and seeing people I have heard about and prayed for, but who seemed no more real than a dream. Now I find that they are real, with lives and loves and hurts.

Elsie—the first Elsie—was a Christian, Mamma, and just my age. She must have known that Cousin Horace did not belong to Jesus, as he is no deceiver, but she married him anyway. Surely she knew Paul's words that I have read over and over again these last weeks, 'Do not be yoked together with unbelievers. For what do righteousness and wickedness have in common? Or what fellowship can light have with darkness? What harmony is there between Christ and Belial? What does a believer have in common with an unbeliever?'

If she had asked the council of the godly women who raised her, would she have chosen another path? These are questions that followed her to the grave, I fear, and I can't know her answers.

But I see the result of her decision—a child who doesn't know the love of her father and a home broken not only by death, but because one spouse did not know life with our beloved Savior. Oh, Mamma, my heart was slipping toward Charles. Could God have brought me here to show me this? Pray that little Elsie's story makes me stronger in my own resolve, for no day passes when Charles Landreth is not in my heart.

As Millie sat at the open window of her dressing room the next morning, enjoying the beauty of the landscape, she heard the patter of little feet in the corridor and then a gentle rap upon her door.

She hurried to open it and found the tiny girl in a spotless white gown trimmed with costly lace. Her slippers matched her pale blue sash, and brown curls clustered about her face. She was holding a beautiful doll whose dress and shoes matched her own.

"Good morning, Cousin," said the little voice. "May I come see you?"

"Of course! And who is this?" Millie asked.

"Sarah," Elsie explained. "She's my best friend, next to Jesus."

"May I see Sarah? I thought you were twins. You dress just alike." Elsie handed over the doll. Millie examined the soft hair and eyes that opened and closed, admiring them aloud. "She's very pretty and delicate!"

"Do you want to come with me to see my Mamma?" Elsie asked when Millie handed the doll back.

"I should like that very much." Millie allowed herself to be led along the corridor and through an open door at its far end. There she found herself in a boudoir furnished in the most luxurious and tasteful manner. She had seen enough of Isabel's ornaments to know that these were extremely costly, though there was nothing gaudy about them. Little Elsie led her to a life-sized picture of a young woman.

"That's her," Elsie whispered. "My sweet Mamma."

Millie studied the beautiful, wistful face. There was something in the eyes and in the small smile that made her sure that they would have been friends.

There were two other portraits in the room, which Elsie said were "Grandpa and Grandma Grayson," a pleasant-looking couple with none of the grimness of the Landreth's dead relations. Elsie pointed out her mother's writing desk and her worktable on which a dainty basket sat. A little gold thimble and a bit of embroidery with the needle still sticking in it could be seen inside.

"Just where my darlin' child laid it down on the day her baby girl was born," Aunt Chloe said, coming into the room.

Little Elsie took Millie's hand and led her on through a beautiful dressing room into a spacious and elegant bedroom, where a Bible sat open on the bedside table.

"That's the very pillow her head lay on," Aunt Chloe said. She began to describe the last hours of her young mistress, and her mournful leave-taking of her little babe. Tears ran down Aunt Chloe's cheeks as she spoke.

Millie fought a sudden urge to throw open the window and let the breeze into the room, to muss the bedclothes and turn the pages of the book that had sat open on the bedside stand for four long years. *Surely the pretty young girl who died here is with Jesus now, not trapped in these sad memories. But four years has not been long enough to heal the heart of the nursemaid who loved her like a daughter.*

"Don't cry, Aunt Chloe!" said Elsie, pulling her down into a chair and laying Sarah on the floor so she could use her own tiny white handkerchief to wipe away Aunt Chloe's tears. "Don't cry. Mamma is happy with Jesus."

At that, Aunt Chloe hugged the tiny child to her chest with a fresh burst of sobs, and looking up at Millie with big tears rolling down her cheeks, she said, "Miss Millie, your uncle ain't gonna take my child away from me, is he? She's all I got left to love in this world."

"No! Uncle Horace has assured me you will not be parted," assured Millie.

"Oh! That is blessed news! There, there, don't cry, it'll come out right," she said as she rocked little Elsie. But her eyes went to the empty bed and Millie was not quite sure if she was talking to the little girl or herself.

At that moment a bell rang.

"Breakfast is ready," Elsie said, patting Aunt Chloe's hand. She led the way to the dining room. Uncle Horace was in an excellent mood, having spent the morning perusing the financial records. He spoke of the output of the sugarhouse, shipping considerations, the efficiency of the operation, and how production could be improved.

"I am not finished with the books," he said at last. "Will you join me in going over them, or would you prefer to spend the time getting to know Elsie?"

"I believe I will spend the day with Elsie," Millie said, relieved that she had an excuse that would free her to explore the plantation at leisure.

Millie soon found that it was Aunt Chloe who planned Elsie's days, taking her on long walks and dictating her nap times. Mrs. Murray loved the child just as dearly, and the two of them seemed like maiden aunts raising a foundling child. At times they were at odds over what was best for her noon meal, or whether she should take a nap. But between them, Millie was sure no child had ever been more loved or fussed over. Sarah went everywhere in the house with the child, with the exception of the dining table. When Elsie went outside, she put Sarah carefully to sleep in a bassinet that must have been her own when she was tiny.

This morning, while Mrs. Murray set the household staff in order and gave them their directions, Aunt Chloe suggested a walk to the quarters. After Sarah was tucked into bed, Elsie held Millie's hand to show her the way.

The little girl was apparently much at home in the slaves' quarters, unlike Louise and Lora, who had never visited the quarters at Roselands. Elsie ran to play with the little children, accepting a corn cake from an elderly woman with a toothless smile and sharing it with a roly-poly baby boy who called her 'Ci-ci' and shouted for more when the treat was gone. Elsie patted his cheeks and gave him a kiss, but he only yelled louder.

"Aunt Chloe," called a young woman with a basket of laundry from the big house balanced on her hip. Her eyes went to Millie briefly, and then back to the more familiar face. "What's gonna happen, do ya know?"

Aunt Chloe shook her head. "You think I can just ask things like that, Rilla? We have to wait and see."

"I've got a baby on the way, miss." Rilla looked at Millie. "I have to know if we's gonna be sold. I don't want to be parted from my man."

"I . . . I don't know," Millie said. She had never considered the worry the slaves must be feeling over the death of little Elsie's guardian. If Viamede was to be sold, they could be put to auction and their families split up. The whole little community—with friends, married couples, children, and grandparents—could be separated, never to see or hear of one another again. They must have been waiting in terrible anxiety ever since they learned of his death.

"I will ask my uncle tonight," Millie promised. "And Aunt Chloe will let you know."

Millie brought the slaves' concerns up with her uncle that afternoon.

"You can assure them that no one will be sold, unless they are unruly or disobedient," Uncle Horace said. "Viamede will continue to be a working plantation until my son decides what is to be done with it. I will hire a manager to control it in his absence."

Millie conveyed this information to Aunt Chloe, who hurried to spread the news through the community. Mrs. Murray confessed that she, too, feared separation from "the bairn I've learned to love as my very own."

Millie's Faithful Heart

This time, when Millie went to inquire of her uncle, he dropped his pen in exasperation. "Why do they not just ask me?"

"They are, no doubt, put off by the light cheerfulness of your countenance and manner," Millie said. "To say nothing of the gentle tone of your voice."

"That is a good point," he said, picking up the pen and stretching his lips to practice a smile. "You may ask Mrs. Murray if she would be interested in taking the position of housekeeper at Roselands for a year. Mrs. Brown informed me before we left that her health was failing and she must resign her situation for a year or more."

"Would you be willing to travel to Roselands and leave your home at Viamede?" Millie asked the housekeeper later.

"The bairn is far dearer to me than the place," Mrs. Murray said, "though I have spent the best years of my life here. I have a mother's heart for her, Miss Keith." Mrs. Murray suggested that Aunt Phyllis, an old servant in the family, be left in charge of the mansion, and Uncle Horace took her advice.

The affairs of the plantation were in such good order that it required only Uncle Horace hiring a manager to be left in charge before they could start on their way. His solicitor had recommended three, and Uncle Horace interviewed them all and chose the one he felt most competent in business and in character. The man seemed to get along well with the servants and slaves, and everyone was well-pleased.

"It must be hard for you to leave this lovely place," Millie said to Mrs. Murray on the eve of their departure.

"I can't deny that it is," the housekeeper answered with a sigh, "for I have lived at Viamede many years in which I have seen much of both joy and sorrow. I had hoped to end my days here. But may the Lord's will be done."

Elsie herself was the last one to learn of her departure. Uncle Horace called the child to him and sat her in a very businesslike manner on a chair. Millie was pleased to see that he was attempting a smile. Elsie looked at him uncertainly. Her dainty little shoes stuck straight out in front of her, and she folded her hands in her lap.

"Now then," he said. "You must prepare yourself for a trip. Do you understand?"

"Yes. What's a trip?" the little girl asked.

"We are going to leave Viamede," he explained, "and travel a very long time, and finally we will be at Roselands, your father's home."

"Is my Pappa there?" asked Elsie.

"No," Uncle Horace said. "Your Pappa is currently in Europe."

"Syrup?" Elsie said with a puzzled frown.

"Millie," Uncle Horace said. "Can you explain? I have never been able to communicate with children!"

Millie knelt by the chair. "Would you like to travel to your Pappa's home?" she asked. "There are little boys and girls there to play with. There is Enna, who is just a baby girl, only two years old."

"I'm four," Elsie said. "I'm a big girl."

"Yes, and you will have to be very kind to Enna and share your toys. Walter is four, nearly as old as you. And Adelaide is a very big girl. She is waiting to meet you already."

Elsie considered it for a moment. "Will Sarah come, too?"

Uncle Horace looked to Millie for clarification. "Her doll," Millie explained.

"Sarah is certainly welcome," Uncle Horace said.

Millie's Faithful Heart

"Then I will go," Elsie decided.

When the time came for the final parting, the house servants gathered around Elsie, weeping. She embraced them in turn, clinging about their necks. Though she was too young to understand that she might not see them again, she had a tender heart and their tears brought tears to her own eyes. Aunt Phyllis was sobbing, and this upset Elsie most of all. "Don't cry," she kept saying, patting the woman's face and kissing her. "Don't cry, Aunt Phyllis. I'll be home soon."

"Come, come," Uncle Horace said at last. "We have had enough of this. There's no use in crying over what can't be helped. The boat is waiting and the captain wanting to be off."

"Yes, Mr. Dinsmore," Mrs. Murray said, wiping her eyes.

"Then let us go on board." He started to take his little granddaughter in his arms, but Aunt Phyllis, who was being left behind, begged the privilege of carrying her to the pier. Uncle Horace was left to carry Sarah, as everyone else had their arms full.

When they reached the pier, Aunt Phyllis gave little Elsie one last embrace, and then resigned her to her nursemaid.

"There, honey, dry your eyes and be brave," Aunt Chloe said, standing on the deck and lifting the child high in her arms as the boat pulled away from the pier. "Look! Everyone's standing to wave you goodbye."

Elsie stretched out her arms to her home and her friends with a cry. Then, as the boat swept onward, she turned and buried her face in Aunt Chloe's bosom. The riverboat caught the current and the paddle began to churn, carrying them back to Roselands. *Back to Charles.*

CHAPTER

13

A Mixed Reception

"Whoever welcomes one of these little children in my name welcomes me; and whoever welcomes me does not welcome me but the one who sent me."

MARK 9:37

A Mixed Reception

On the very first morning of their trip, Millie learned, to her delight, that Elsie was an early riser, too. The little girl crawled onto Millie's lap as she read her Bible. She listened intently as Millie read, pointing to words and asking, "What's that one say?"

Millie made a game of teaching Elsie her letters as she read each morning, and soon there were a few simple words that Elsie could recognize by sight. The little girl would clap her hands with delight when she found the word *Jesus*, *God*, or *Lord* on a page.

"I'm reading," she would inform Aunt Chloe or Mrs. Murray as she turned the pages.

Sarah, the little girl's constant companion, proved a difficult traveler. Although her wardrobe had been neatly folded and packed in Elsie's bags, her bassinet was too large to travel. This caused "trouble" when it came to Sarah's taking her naps on the paddleboat. "Sarah misses her own bed," Elsie said, hugging the doll. "She can't sleep."

"If she will be patient, we might make her a very special bed when we reach New Orleans," Millie promised. The stop of a few days in New Orleans allowed Uncle Horace to buy gifts for the family and Millie to procure what was needed for the doll. Uncle Horace was happy to purchase fabric, needles, thread, and a basket for Millie to work with. The work of a few hours produced a perfect satin and lace basket bed for Elsie's baby.

Millie requested one more thing from Uncle Horace; a small, black pocket Bible was purchased—just the right size for Elsie's tiny hands. Millie's own Bible was practically falling apart, and use by even the most careful four-year-old would be a hazard to its loose pages.

In the mornings following its purchase, Elsie sat primly beside Millie with her own little Bible open, pretending to read as Millie read. She carried her Bible with her in a tiny reticule, just like Millie's larger one.

Millie had ample time during the weeks of travel to get to know her little cousin, and soon came to the conclusion that little Elsie simply had a sweet and biddable nature. It was God's grace that had given her into the care of two such women as Mrs. Murray and Aunt Chloe—both strong, godly women with years of experience in bringing up a child. Elsie's nature would surely have been very different if she had been left to the care of someone such as Isabel.

Millie spent a great deal of time praying for Cousin Horace and his little girl. *Would Cousin Horace be a Christian today if his young wife had lived?* There were so many questions that would never be answered. Millie spent a great deal of time thinking about Charles, too. She searched her Bible daily, looking for any Scripture that would imply that loving Charles was a sin, but could not find one. Jesus loved Charles, too.

Then why, why, why could it possibly be wrong to marry him? And yet the Bible was clear that it was. Millie began to feel like the midnight friend from chapter eleven of the book of Luke, banging on the door of heaven and asking for an answer over and over again.

Then one morning as Millie was reading the book of Acts, it was as if God spoke clearly to her heart. She had just read the passage in Acts 7 in which Stephen preached God's Word to the Sanhedrin. Of course, he must have hoped that they would believe in Jesus and be saved. But they did not. They decided to kill him, and "the witnesses laid their clothes at the feet of a young man named Saul." The very same Saul who would later become the great apostle Paul!

Was Stephen the first Christian that Saul had ever seen? What if Stephen had denied Jesus? But he did not. He preached God's Word faithfully, and he died without betraying his Lord. Saul did not become a Christian that day, or for several years. But surely God used the seeds that were planted by Stephen's faithfulness that day. God sent Stephen to preach the Good News to Saul. Did God send me to Roselands to tell Charles the truth? To live the truth so that he could know it was real?

"Millie, why are you crying?" Elsie asked, wrapping her arms around Millie's neck.

"God is just watering my heart," Millie said, "so that the love in it will grow bigger."

The Roselands plantation was in glorious late spring bloom when the weary travelers returned. Millie could not help but think of Laylie as they rolled up the drive. *Is she in New York by now, or some other northern state, safe and free? Will I ever know?* Laylie and Luke had been much on her mind, and it was difficult not to speak to anyone about them. Millie prayed for both of them daily, and she prayed now, asking God to keep them safe wherever they were. She was still praying silently when the stagecoach stopped. Someone had seen the stagecoach coming and spread the news. Even Isabel was waiting on the steps. There was a tumultuous embracing of their father and Cousin Millie by the children.

"Father's making a funny face," Walter said.

"That's not a face," Adelaide informed her brother. "He's smiling."

"I have been practicing," Uncle Horace said, winking at Millie. "Just for you, my boy!" Walter smiled back and wrapped his arms around his father's knee. There were more hugs all around, and then the Dinsmore children turned their attention to the newcomer who looked down at them, half shy and half eager, from Aunt Chloe's arms.

"Oh, you darling," cried Adelaide, reaching her with a bound and giving her a vigorous hug and kiss. "Do you know that I'm your auntie? Don't you think it's funny?" The embrace was instantly returned, a beautiful smile breaking over little Elsie's face. Millie smiled, too. Here was one friend for Elsie, at least.

"Don't tease the child, Adelaide. Let her alone," Isabel said sharply.

No one seemed to hear Isabel's command. The children and servants gathered round, examining Elsie with as much curiosity as if she were a new toy, the girls remarking upon the beauty of her complexion, her eyes, and her hair.

"They'll have the bairn fairly puffed up with vanity, Miss Millie!" exclaimed Mrs. Murray in a dismayed tone.

"Never mind," whispered Millie, "I'm glad she should have such a welcome to her new home."

"There, children, that will do," Uncle Horace said with authority. "The child is tired from her long journey. Carry her to her room, Aunt Chloe, and let her have something to eat and a nap."

"Yes, sir," Aunt Chloe said, picking Elsie up again. "Which way is it?"

"I'll show you," Mrs. Brown said. Millie picked up Elsie's baby basket and followed them down the hall. She was a little surprised when Mrs. Brown led the way past the family's quarters and the comfortable apartments she herself occupied, toward the back of the house.

The housekeeper stopped at last and pushed open a door. The small room that was revealed was nothing more than a maid's room. It was immaculately clean, and someone had tried to brighten it with a vase of flowers. But the small bed and plain white curtains could not hide the fact that it was part of the servants' quarters.

"*This* is my little missus's room?" Aunt Chloe asked in disbelief.

"I'm sure there has been some mistake," Millie said. "I will speak to my uncle. Wait a moment before you unpack her bags." Elsie herself was looking around the room with big eyes. The child was too small to understand that it was not a pleasant or even a very nice room that she had been given, but she could feel the tension in her nursemaid's arms.

Millie found Uncle Horace still in the parlor with his family about him. Isabel was holding up the lovely jeweled bracelet he had purchased for her in New Orleans for everyone to admire.

"Is the child suitably settled?" Uncle Horace asked, looking to Millie.

"I'm afraid not," Millie said. "There has been a mistake about her room."

"What kind of mistake?"

"She has been put in the servants' quarters."

"What?" Uncle Horace came to his feet. "Excuse me, my dear," he gave Isabel a kiss. "I will return in a moment." He followed Millie down the hall to the small room where Mrs. Brown, Aunt Chloe, and Elsie were waiting.

"What are you doing in this pigeon hole, Mrs. Brown?" he exclaimed. "Who told you to bring Horace Jr.'s daughter here?"

"Mrs. Dinsmore instructed us to prepare this room for the child," Mrs. Brown said. "She said the child and her nurse would take their meals with us in the kitchen."

"You must have misunderstood her," Uncle Horace said, flushing. "Come this way, Aunt Chloe."

He led the way to the room adjoining Millie's, which was very large, airy, cheerful, and well furnished. "I think this one will do nicely," he said.

"Horace, what are you doing?" Isabel, who was still shaking her arm to make the jewels flash, had followed him at last.

"My dear," he said, "someone mistook your orders and prepared a cubbyhole for Horace's child. You need not concern yourself. I have accepted full responsibility for the child, and that includes choosing her rooms."

"There was no mistake," Isabel said. "I felt the little room was quite nice for a Grayson. I wanted her to feel at home, and not out of her element." Aunt Chloe held Elsie closer and threw a worried look at Millie.

"She is a Dinsmore," Uncle Horace said. "And born in a palace. But more than that, she is my grandchild, and heiress in her own right to a great fortune."

Isabel looked astonished. "A fortune? I never dreamed . . . Still, you simply cannot put her in the blue room. The satin damask cushions of the chairs and sofas are so handsome and delicate! Think of a baby rubbing its shoes over them and scattering greasy crumbs on that exquisite carpet!"

"She is a very careful child. It is hardly more comfortable than the room she left at Viamede. But don't distress yourself over furniture," Uncle Horace took her in his arms. "Her income is quite sufficient to allow this room to be refurnished at double the cost every six months if necessary."

"Really?" Isabel looked around. "Fine. Then have her things brought here. I was only thinking of her comfort, Horace."

"Of course you were," Uncle Horace said.

"Oh, and Millie, there have been letters for you from home. I put them in the top drawer in your room," said Aunt Isabel.

Millie practically ran to the room. The first letter from her mother had been sent before Uncle Horace's message about little Elsie reached Pleasant Plains. It was full of news about the plans for Damaris's wedding, with expressions of delight that Adelaide would be coming to visit. Her mother expressed that Zillah was most eager for Millie's return, or if not Millie herself, at least her wardrobe.

The second letter was dated mid-April, after Millie's letter had arrived. It was obvious from its brevity that her mother was guarding her words.

Dearest Daughter,

Your Pappa and I have discussed the matter and he is coming himself to bring you home. Your visit to Roselands, while it sounds delightful in many respects, has been quite long enough, and after your trip to Viamede, we cannot expect your Uncle Horace to leave his family for yet another cross-country journey.

Millie's Faithful Heart

You may expect Pappa the first week of June. As always, we know you will honor us, and more importantly, Jesus, in all your decisions. There is so much more I would like to say to you, but there will be time, darling. Know that you are in all of our prayers night and day, until you are home.

Pappa will be here any day! He must have left as soon as they received my letter—it would have been on its way a month. Millie took the letter to her Uncle Horace. Isabel already knew, of course, but would pretend it was a surprise.

"I cannot say that I am sorry that I won't be making another trip," Uncle Horace said. "Though we will be losing you sooner than I had hoped."

"And I cannot say that I am not eager to return home," Millie laughed. "I have missed my family more than I can say."

Millie put her letter in her pocket and went to give her cousins a proper greeting at last. She found them in the nursery, busy with the toys their father had brought them. They all wanted to hear the story of her journey and were fascinated by the pictures in her sketchbook. They were still trying to guess what some of her sketches were when Elsie, fresh from her nap, arrived with Aunt Chloe.

"You are the darlingest little thing!" Adelaide said, catching her in her arms and kissing her.

"She's too pretty. Nobody will ever look at us when she's near. I heard Mother say so," muttered Louise. "I wish she would go back where she came from."

"What's the use of talking that way?" said Lora. "We can hide her upstairs when we want to be looked at."

"I'm her uncle!" Arthur said, drawing himself up with dignity. "Say 'Uncle Arthur's baby girl.'"

"I'm not the baby," Elsie said. "Enna's the baby."

Walter, who was just a little taller than Elsie even though he was a bit younger, had not said a word since she arrived. He walked up to her now and held out his favorite toy, a red and yellow top. "I wike you," he said.

"Well, well," Aunt Chloe said. "Maybe things will work out after all. Maybe they will."

CHAPTER 14

The Truest Love

*It is better, if it is God's will,
to suffer for doing good
than for doing evil.*

1 Peter 3:17

*C*harles arrived the next afternoon with a bouquet for Isabel and a dozen red roses for Millie. Millie sent up a quick prayer for courage as soon as he was announced. "Will you take a walk with me in the garden?" Millie asked, after he had exchanged pleasantries with Horace and Isabel.

"I would be delighted," he said. "Though I am usually the one who asks!"

"Wait for me for just one moment," Millie said. She went to her room for her Bible and then met Charles on the step. They walked through the garden, Millie not quite sure how to begin.

"Let's stop here," Charles said, and Millie realized it was the same tree under which he had proposed months ago. She felt a blush creeping into her cheeks.

"I take this as a very good sign," Charles said, smiling. "Have you discovered that you cannot live without me?"

"Charles Landreth, I do love you. With all my heart," she sighed. Charles took a step nearer and reached for her hand. The blush was surely gone, for Millie was feeling chilled now. She had to finish quickly or she would forget what she had to say. "I love you far too well to marry you."

"What?" Charles shook his head. "That makes no sense, Millie. None."

"It only makes sense if God is real, and Jesus is His Son. God's Word says that I can't marry you, Charles. And I will do anything—even live without you—to prove to you that God's Word is true. Jesus is worth living for. And dying for.

Millie's Faithful Heart

You need His love much more than you need mine. And there is nothing that can change my mind."

"You are throwing away our love because of stories in a book?" His face was pale. "For fairy tales?"

"No," Millie said. "I am obeying the Living God. He's real, and He cares about you more than I ever could. I know it is hard to understand, but my life belongs to Him."

"Then there is not much more to say."

"Charles, if you truly love me, I want you to take this." She held out her Bible. "It is the most precious thing I own." Charles took the Bible gingerly. "You have to be careful with it," Millie said. "The pages have started falling out."

"You might as well keep it," his voice was bitter. "I won't read it."

Millie shook her head. "I want you to have it. I want you to remember me. And Charles . . . the Savior it describes in that book — He is what my life is all about. If you love me, maybe He has something to do with it. Maybe you are seeing Jesus in me."

Charles looked as if he wished he could throw the Bible across the garden, but he tucked it under his arm instead.

"Goodbye, Millie Keith," he said. "I can show myself out."

Millie sank down to the ground, drawing her knees up under her chin. She sat for a long time under the tree, but strangely, this time the tears wouldn't come. Aunt Isabel was waiting when she came in.

"You are a stupid, stupid young woman," she said. "Don't you know that you are letting the opportunity of a lifetime walk away?"

Millie stopped. "I am showing the man I love what true love is."

"You will change your mind, I believe, before you leave. I will invite Charles to my dinner party in two weeks, after this has had a chance to blow over."

"A party that I will not attend. Aunt Isabel, Laylie is gone. You have nothing to hold over me now. You can stop trying to be a matchmaker. Jesus is the only one I trust with something as important as my heart."

"Well, this Jesus of yours was either not watching, or didn't listen when you asked him to keep your heart." Isabel had the decency to flush, realizing she had given herself away. There was no way she could have known this without reading Millie's diary.

Millie looked her in the eye. "You were wrong to read my diary, and you were wrong to read my letters," she said. "You will not do it again, or I will explain to Uncle Horace exactly how you conduct yourself toward his guests."

"Is that a threat?" she asked.

"It's a promise," Millie said. "And when I make a promise, or an agreement of any kind, I keep it."

"How dare you! I believe I have a perfect right to see what kind of people are staying in my home, in whatever way . . . " Millie turned her back on her and walked away. She stopped in the entryway and chose just one of Charles's roses to take with her to her room. She pinned it upside down on the window side of the curtain, where it could dry in the sun.

The next morning when little Elsie arrived promptly at dawn to read the Bible, Millie pulled her up onto her lap.

"May we read from your little Bible today?" Millie asked.

Millie's Faithful Heart

Elsie pulled it from her pocket and together they read Jeremiah 29:11. "'For I know the plans I have for you', declares the Lord, 'plans to prosper you and not to harm you, plans to give you hope and a future.'" Then Elsie left to put Sarah to bed before they went to the nursery to have breakfast with the Dinsmore children.

Jesus, Millie prayed when the little girl was gone, *You know how Aunt Isabel has treated me. You know how she will treat Your sweet little Elsie. Please protect Your lamb. Be her heavenly Pappa while her earthly Pappa is not here. Thank You for giving her Aunt Chloe and Mrs. Murray, for their daily guidance in her life. Protect them, too. I do not know why You brought little Elsie here, but I trust You, Lord. Guard her heart, dear Lord. Keep it pure.*

Life at Roselands quickly settled back into a normal routine. Every morning Millie woke with the tickly feeling that something was going to happen. *Could this be the day that Pappa will arrive?* After breakfast Millie would take a horseback ride or sit in the garden sketching the early summer blossoms, as the feeling of anticipation grew. *Surely today will be the day Pappa will take me away from Roselands, from Aunt Isabel, and the constant reminders of Charles.* Every room, every corner of the garden, was haunted by memories of his laughter and his smiles. Millie knew she had done the right thing, but that didn't make it hurt any less. The ache was constant.

Millie was at the foot of the garden one day when a pebble bounced off of her sketchbook.

"Psst, miss!"

She looked up to see a pair of brown eyes peering at her from the bushes.

"It's me, miss. Little John. Robin said for you to come with me."

Laylie? Millie tucked her book under her arm and followed the child into the woods. Laylie was standing outside the Merry Men's hut. She was dirty and thin, and there were dark circles under her eyes. Millie gathered her up in her arms and hugged her till she squeaked.

"Put me down," Laylie said. "You hug too tight!"

"What on earth are you doing back at Roselands?" Millie asked, setting her on her feet. "And where is Luke?"

"Right here, miss," came a voice from the small hut. Millie ducked inside and saw Luke leaning against the rock that formed the back of the hut, his legs stretched out in front of him. There were rags tied around his feet, stained with what could only be blood.

"What happened?" Millie said, dropping to her knees.

"Got caught," Luke explained. " 'Bout eight nights after we got off that train, by a man named Cyrus. He didn't have slaves of his own, but he had the chains. Ouch! Those rags are stuck on, miss." The rags appeared to be shreds of Laylie's petticoat, and they were indeed stuck to the bottom of his injured feet.

"He made Luke work," Laylie said, crawling in beside Millie. "But I prayed to Jesus to help us get away. We were there a long time, maybe a month. Then one day Old Cyrus went to sleep and I took the key to the chains. He kept it on his belt. It wasn't stealing, 'cause I left it after I used it."

"What happened to Luke's feet?" Millie knew she would need warm water and soap to remove the bandages.

"Cyrus had a horse," Laylie said. "When he woke up, he came after us. Luke picked me up and ran."

"Woods slowed the horse down some," Luke said. "We stuck to the woods."

"He just kept runnin' and runnin'," Laylie said, "and he wouldn't put me down."

"Your legs is too short. Ouch! *Please* don't touch me, miss!" he said.

"Well, you are not running for a while," Millie said, giving up on examining the feet. "I don't see how you can walk on these."

"He did walk, for days and days," Laylie said. "We found the ocean and started following the North Star. It's easier to find food and water by the ocean. Sometimes I caught fish, and Luke, he dug for clams. All the creeks run to the ocean sometime, so we had water. We've been three weeks coming."

"She wouldn't steal nothin'. She said King Jesus wouldn't like it," Luke said accusingly. "We near starved."

"Yesterday, I figured out we were close to Roselands. I saw the tree over the cliff where we used to sit, and the place where the ocean writes poems. I knew I had to come here, Millie. Luke needs help."

"I told her not to come here," Luke frowned at his sister. "People here know us. It's the worst place we can be. But I couldn't move fast enough to stop her, so I had to come along."

"Have you eaten today?" Millie asked.

"The Merry Men brought us food," Laylie said. "It was their own dinner."

Millie nodded. "Luke is right, Laylie. This is a very bad place for you to be."

"But . . . you can help his feet, Millie?" the young girl looked up pleadingly.

"I'll go to Old Rachel," Millie decided. "I don't know if she will help, but I don't think she will turn you in."

Millie hoped she sounded calm when she asked Ajax to saddle a horse for her. "I will be going to Ion for a visit," she explained, even though Ajax didn't ask.

As soon as she was out of sight of the big house, Millie kicked the horse to a gallop. When she reached Ion, she didn't wait for the stable hand to lift her down, but slid off the saddle and tossed him the reins as she ran for the front steps.

"Mrs. Travilla is away visiting," the servant informed her.

"I'm here to see Old Rachel," Millie explained.

The man merely inclined his head. "This way, miss." He led her to the parlor where she had visited before, and offered her a chair. Millie watched the hands on the clock slide slowly past the hour as she waited. Finally, she heard steps in the hall.

"Miss Millie!" Old Rachel said, entering the room. "I'm just pleased as peas to see you. I thought you had gone away down south." The servant stood by the door, pretending to ignore Millie.

"I traveled with Uncle Horace to New Orleans," Millie explained. She stopped, groping for words.

"Now I know that's not what you come to say," the old woman prompted.

Millie looked at the servant. "Could you . . . leave us?"

"As you wish, miss," he said. She waited until his footsteps faded down the hall.

"It's about Luke and Laylie," Millie began.

"Luke? The dead boy?" Old Rachel leaned forward as Millie began to tell the story, starting with the discovery that Luke was alive. Rachel tsked and clucked now and then until the story was over. Then she just sat looking at Millie.

"I need help," Millie said.

"Well, I guess you do," Old Rachel agreed. "But I'm not the one who can give it." She started to stand up. Millie's face must have reflected her distress, because the old woman said, "I didn't say I didn't know where to get it. Come on." Millie followed Rachel down the halls to her own small room. There Rachel chose a thin book from a shelf of well-worn volumes. "You take this to Mr. Blessed Bliss. Tell him that Old Rachel is returning his book after all these years."

Millie looked down at the book. It was a thin volume of poetry. "Blessed Bliss? Are you sure?"

"Sure as sure can be." Old Rachel picked up her bonnet and put it over her thin white hair. "I will go take care of that boy's feet while you do. And Miss Millie?"

"Yes?"

"I saw the way you come tearing up the drive. Don't you go to town that way. Folks might think there was something wrong. You go back to Roselands, get pretty, and go into town for some shopping."

"Yes, ma'am," Millie said with a faint smile.

⸻

"Why, Millie Keith!" Miz Opal said, when Millie walked in the door. "I thought you had gone away!"

"I did take a trip," Millie said, "and returned only days ago. Is Mr. Bliss here?"

"Mr. Bliss?" Miz Opal said in surprise. "I suppose he is. Is everyone well at Roselands?"

"Quite well," Millie said. "I have something to return to him."

"I think he may be in the kitchen. Just follow me." Miz Opal led the way past the coffin and chairs, through the back door of the shop, and into the small kitchen.

Mr. Bliss was in the kitchen in much the same pose Millie had seen him on her previous visit—perched on the edge of a chair listening to the Colonel, who seemed to be telling the story of a river race on the Amazon. Dearest was rolling piecrust on the table. She had put on a white apron to keep the flour from dusting her widow's weeds, and her veil was thrown back over her head. It was the first time Millie had seen her without her veil obscuring her face, which turned out to be plump and cheerful.

"Our friend from the ship!" she cried when they entered. "How marvelous!"

The Colonel rolled his eyes. He had obviously given up explaining the difference between ships and boats to Dearest.

Millie took out the thin book and handed it to Mr. Bliss, feeling foolish even as she did it. "Old Rachel is returning your book at last."

Blessed Bliss turned the book over slowly and then looked up at Millie. "You have someone who needs our help," he said in his deep, funeral parlor voice. Millie glanced at the Colonel.

"Have no fear of speaking here, young lady," Mr. Bliss said, offering her his chair. "You are among friends." Millie

began again, explaining the story just as she had to Old Rachel.

"They rode the *Phoenix*!" the Colonel said when her story was done. "That is marvelous! And now to the rescue! The young man can't walk you say. We will need a wagon, or a camel. I remember a time in the Sahara . . ."

"Not now, Colonel," Blessed said. "I need to think."

"We could take them with us to New York, pretending they were our slaves," Miz Opal said. "If only people here didn't know them. We can't risk them being seen by someone who knew them at Roselands."

"Pop him in a coffin," the Colonel suggested. "I once smuggled a princess out of Cairo in a gold sarcophagus . . ."

"That was a story in the last issue of *Ladies Weekly Miscellany*, Colonel," Miz Opal said. "It was completely fictional."

"But . . . it might work." Blessed started to pace. "He would have to have food, of course, but once on the ship you could let him out now and then. Change ships at the next harbor and he could travel as your servant from that point on!"

Dearest clapped her hands. "The young girl can be an orphan! I'm sure she'd make a lovely orphan!"

"Won't people find it a little odd?" Millie asked. "Miz Opal and the Colonel leaving town with a coffin and an orphan?"

"We are the Blisses," Dearest said, patting her hand. "Nothing we do surprises people anymore."

"The first thing to do is get them here," Miz Opal said sensibly. Everyone looked at Millie.

"Aunt Isabel is having a dinner party tomorrow night," Millie said. "There will be coaches and carriages all along

the drive. If you could bring your carriage then, I'm sure Luke and Laylie could slip into it in the dark."

After the plans were made and remade, Miz Opal walked Millie to the door. "I know Blessed and the Colonel are not what you were expecting when you went to Old Rachel, dear," she said. "They hardly seem to be the heroic type. But God does use the foolish things of the world to confound the wise. It doesn't matter who we are really — just who He is. If I have learned one thing in this life, it is this: 'We can do everything through Him who gives us strength.' "

The door shut behind her and Millie shook her head. "You have the strangest friends, Lord," she whispered, looking up and smiling toward heaven.

Millie's head was throbbing the next morning. It was the result of staying up half the night talking to Laylie in the woods, and the other half praying for their safety, but it gave her the perfect excuse not to attend Isabel's party.

She intended to wait in her room until dark and then slip out to help Laylie get Luke safely to the Bliss's coach. The time could be well spent praying, as she felt that this particular operation needed all of the prayer it could get.

Millie's father spoiled her plans by arriving that very afternoon. He stepped from the stagecoach, gathered Millie in his arms, and held her for a long time before letting her toes touch the ground. "I have just decided that you are never allowed to leave home again," he said. "Unless you take us with you."

"At this moment, I am only too happy to agree, Pappa!" Millie laughed.

The Dinsmore children were watching the tall stranger with a mixture of curiosity and shyness. After Stuart put

Millie's Faithful Heart

Millie down, Elsie slipped her little hand in Millie's and pulled her down to whisper level. "Is that your own dear Pappa?" the little girl asked.

"Yes," said Millie in a soft voice.

"I hope my Pappa picks me up so high my toes don't touch, too," said Elsie.

"I'm sure he will," whispered Millie reassuringly, "as soon as he comes home."

"Is he taking you away, Millie?" asked Adelaide. "I don't want you to go!"

"I promise I will write to you, Adelaide. And I need you to take care of little Elsie for me, until your brother comes home." Adelaide nodded solemnly and took Elsie's hand.

"Stuart, I hope you will be willing to stay a few days and enjoy our hospitality as I enjoyed yours," Uncle Horace said, shaking his hand.

"I wish I was able to," Stuart said. "But we were delayed by a storm and already I am a week later than I had hoped. In fact, I booked passage for tomorrow."

"Then we will entertain you tonight. My wife will be delighted," said Horace.

"Is all well, daughter?" Stuart said, as they walked back toward the house.

"Yes, Pappa. I have so much to tell you."

He squeezed her hand. "There will be time."

But there wasn't time before dinner. There was not time to discuss anything alone.

Stuart, with his stories of the frontier, was the life of the dinner party that night. Charles had declined Isabel's invitation, but Otis hung on Stuart's every word.

Millie was torn between listening to her Pappa's voice and straining to hear the crunch of carriage wheels in the night.

The Truest Love

Has Blessed Bliss brought his carriage? Are Luke and Laylie safely away from Roselands? Or are they huddled under the hedge even now, waiting? Have they been able to make it even that far without my help? Every time the servant opened the door, Millie jumped, expecting the news that they had been found out.

"Millie?" Stuart's voice brought her out of her thoughts. "What did you think of Charleston? Were you able to go to the theater or a concert? Some of the finest orchestras in the world can be heard there, I understand."

"It was delightful," Millie said. "I enjoyed the museum and the waterfront very much. The gardens were fabulous, but Mrs. Breandan had parties planned, so we stayed home at night."

"But that night when you and Charles . . ." Otis's plump fingers went to his lips. "Oops!" he said.

"Night?" Isabel said. "I thought Charles came by on the morning you left Charleston?"

"Oh, dear," Otis said. "He shouldn't have told me not to mention it."

Millie was aware of Uncle Horace's eyes on her, as well as her Pappa's. She was sure her face was brighter than the roses in the centerpiece. *What are they thinking? Proper young ladies do not sneak out with gentlemen at night.* But it was Isabel's gaze that frightened her.

"What night was that, Otis?" Isabel asked.

"The night before they left," Otis said, reddening even more than Millie had. "Charles is going to kill me. I'm so sorry, Millie . . ."

"Were Charles and Millie alone?" asked Isabel, setting her wine glass down.

Millie's heart refused to beat until she heard Otis's answer. *Did he see Luke and Laylie?*

213

Millie's Faithful Heart

"Of course they were alone," Otis said. "We met Millie walking downtown and . . . "

Uncle Horace looked from Millie to his wife. "We will discuss this later," he said. "Family business, dear. We have company."

Millie managed to make it through the rest of the meal and the pleasant conversation afterwards only with the greatest willpower.

"I believe we can talk in the library," Uncle Horace said, when all of the guests were gone. He led the way and Isabel, with an unpleasantly happy expression on her face, brought up the rear.

"First of all, Stuart, I want you to understand that the young man we were referring to, Charles Landreth, is of impeccable character. I cannot imagine that he would do anything to tarnish your daughter's reputation. I know that he holds her in the highest regard. In fact, he wishes to marry her," said Horace.

"I have perfect confidence in my daughter," Stuart assured him.

"Horace, use your brain for once," Isabel said. "It isn't the young man you should be thinking about at all. It's the child, Laylie. That was the night she disappeared, wasn't it? Millie helped her escape; how, I cannot tell you. Charles was just a pawn in her hand. He and Otis knew nothing about why she was out that night. They simply acted as gentlemen, seeing her home. She has stolen from my family, and I demand payment, or I *will* summon the law!"

Uncle Horace looked as if he had been struck. He turned slowly to Millie. "Tell your aunt that you had nothing to do with the slave running away," he said. "I apologize for my wife's accusation . . . "

"No, Uncle." Millie's skin felt cold and her stomach hurt. "Don't apologize. I . . . I did help Laylie and her brother Luke escape." *And they are not two miles from us at this moment. Keep them safe, Lord! Please keep them safe!* "They would have been killed at Meadshead. You know how worried I was about them. I was honest with you all along."

Uncle Horace just looked at her in silence.

"I never lied to you, Uncle Horace," Millie said.

"You simply neglected to tell me the truth. How can you have accepted my hospitality for all of this time, and then steal from my family?"

"Uncle Horace, I am so grateful for your extraordinary kindness and generosity toward me. I did not mean to hurt you. But Aunt Isabel promised—"

"I will pay for the slaves," said Stuart, putting his arm around Millie. "I don't have the funds at the moment, but if you write a bill, I will make sure it is paid in full."

"Don't have the funds?" Isabel looked at her husband. "You seemed very liberal when it came to clothing Millie. Nothing was too good for her. And now they cannot pay? I think we should summon the law, Horace. I . . . I was afraid something was amiss when you brought her into this house, but didn't want to say so at the time."

Uncle Horace's face had its old, stiff look back, as if he had never learned to smile at all, and as if he never would again. "I apologize, Stuart. I obviously have not exerted enough influence on your daughter. I am sorry you will be leaving in the morning, but perhaps it is better that way. Isabel? Shall we?" He left the library and Isabel followed.

Stuart held Millie for a long time after the Dinsmores had left the room. Millie wanted to tell him about Luke and

Laylie in the woods, about the Blisses and Miz Opal, but she didn't dare open her mouth. Not in this house.

"It's going to be all right," he said at last. "We will go home tomorrow."

But it wasn't all right. Millie spent a miserable night tossing and turning on her bed. The words Old Rachel had spoken so long ago turned over and over in her mind: *"That child may end up costing you more than you think."* Well, Laylie had cost her more than she ever imagined. She had not realized how dear her uncle had become to her and how much she respected his opinions. That he should think of her as a thief and a liar was almost unbearable. *But what else could I have done? I could change his mind even now. I know where they are and I could tell him. No! What I did was not wrong, no matter what anyone thinks. No matter what they think of me. I will bear this and more, if only Luke and Laylie can be free!*

"Are you going away?" little Elsie asked the next morning when she found Millie packing the last of her things.

"Yes, dear," Millie said. "I want you to know that I am very proud of you for reading your Bible with me every day. Will you promise that you will always read it?"

"Yes," Elsie said solemnly. "But I need more words."

"That's true," Millie said, giving her a hug. "I am sure Mrs. Murray will help you learn them. And I promise to pray for you every single day!"

"Will you pray for my dear Pappa?" Elsie asked.

"Your dear Pappa, too," Millie assured her. "Every single day."

Millie looked around the room one last time. *It looks just as it did on the day of my arrival, as if my stay has not changed a thing. Has it changed me? Only my heart.*

There was a shadow on the curtain. Millie walked slowly over to it, pulled the curtain back, and unpinned the dried rose.

"That rose is not happy-looking like the roses in the garden," Elsie said.

"But it will last much, much longer than those roses," Millie said, tucking the dried bloom into her pocket.

"All the way home?" Elsie asked.

"All the way home and even longer," Millie said.

The little girl followed Millie to the front porch, where Stuart was waiting. There, she took her place by Adelaide, the only Dinsmore child awake to see them leave. Horace and Isabel stood side by side on the porch. Uncle Horace did not shake Stuart's hand and he refused Millie's attempt to hug him goodbye. His face seemed to have settled into its old, wooden form. "Have a safe journey," he said formally.

"Thank you again for everything," Millie said sincerely. Uncle Horace turned and walked away, not willing to meet her eyes.

"Marcia and I will always be grateful for your hospitality to our daughter," Stuart added.

"Remember you promised to write to me!" called Adelaide as Millie stepped into the carriage, but Isabel took Adelaide's hand and called out, "Do *not* write to my children. They do not need the influence of your kind."

Millie leaned against her Pappa's shoulder and cried all the way to town. She craned her neck, trying to see into Blessed Bliss's funeral home as the carriage rolled by, but the curtains were drawn. *Did Blessed find Luke and Laylie? Are they safe, or still huddled in the woods, an impossible distance from freedom?*

Two tall ships lay at anchor—the *Valiant*, a schooner headed for New York, and the *Columbine*, a cutter on its way to Philadelphia. The Keiths' trunks were taken aboard the *Columbine*.

Millie was surprised and touched when Ajax turned and waved before he snapped the reins and started the carriage on its way back to Roselands. Millie and Stuart stood against the rail, watching the other passengers board.

"What are you thinking, daughter?"

"There's so much to say, Pappa, so much to tell you. It's going to take days and days for it all to come out of my heart."

"Well," he said, "I have days and days to listen. God was with you and He kept you safe. We have much to be thankful for."

Suddenly, a funeral procession—a coffin on a hearse, with a child in mourning clothes and veil riding beside it—came around the corner. Four sailors helped lift the coffin from the hearse and carry it up the gangplank of the *Valiant*. The child followed behind, then a matronly woman leaning on the arm of a balding little man.

"We have so much to be thankful for," Pappa repeated, obviously touched by the mourning child's grief. "God is sending you home to us safely."

A tall, thin man in black and his wife, obviously in mourning too, stood waving goodbye as the gangplank was raised.

"If we had known about Isabel, Millie . . . about how things are here . . . we would never have allowed you to come to Roselands. It has changed since your mother's visit so many years ago."

"Pappa," Millie said, lifting her hand in a salute to the mourners, "I would not have missed coming. Not for anything. Some of the most wonderful people in the world live in the South. People of courage and conviction, leading quiet lives of faith. I will never, never forget them."

Just then their ship began to move. Millie stood by her father's side as they left the harbor behind. The sails filled with a wind fresh from the open sea, and the ship began to dance among the waves.

"Goodbye, Charles," Millie whispered. "May God guide your steps, and open your eyes and heart to see His truth."

Will Millie ever hear from Charles again?
Will she ever see Laylie again?
Will Luke and Laylie make it safely to New York?

Find out in:

MILLIE'S STEADFAST LOVE

Book Five
of the
A Life of Faith:
Millie Keith Series

Collect our other
A Life of Faith Products

A Life of Faith: Elsie Dinsmore Series

Published by Mission City Press, Inc.

— ABOUT THE AUTHOR —

*M*artha Finley was born on April 26, 1828, in Chillicothe, Ohio. Her mother died when Martha was quite young, and Dr. James Finley, her father, soon remarried. Martha's stepmother, Mary Finley, was a kind and caring woman who always nurtured Martha's desire to learn and supported her ambition to become a writer.

Dr. Finley was a physician and a devout Christian gentleman. He moved his family to South Bend, Indiana, in the mid-1830s in hopes of a brighter future for his family on the expanding western frontier. Growing up on the frontier as one of eight brothers and sisters surely provided the setting and likely many of the characters for Miss Finley's *Mildred Keith* novels. Considered by many to be partly autobiographical, the books present a fascinating and devoted Christian heroine in the fictional character known as Millie Keith. One can only speculate exactly how much of Martha may have been Millie and vice versa. But regardless, these books nicely complement Miss Finley's bestselling *Elsie Dinsmore* series, which was launched in 1868 and sold millions of copies. The stories of Millie Keith, Elsie's second cousin, were released eight years after the *Elsie* books as a follow-up to that series.

Martha Finley never married and never had children of her own, but she was a remarkable woman who lived a quiet life of creativity and Christian charity. She died at age 81, having written many novels, stories, and books for children and adults. Her life on earth ended in 1909, but her legacy lives on in the wonderful stories of Millie and Elsie.

223

Check out
www.alifeoffaith.com

- Get news about Millie and her cousin Elsie
- Find out more about the 19th century world they live in
- Learn to live a life of faith like they do
- Learn how they overcome the difficulties we all face in life
- Find out about Millie and Elsie products
- Join our girls' club

A Life of Faith Books
"It's Like Having a Best Friend From Another Time"